survival
of the
GINNEST

aimee HOrTON

velvet morning
press

Published by Velvet Morning Press

Copyright © 2015 by Aimee Horton

This is a work of fiction. Names, characters, businesses, places, events and incidents are either the products of the author's imagination or used in a fictitious manner. Any resemblance to actual persons, living or dead, or actual events is purely coincidental.

ISBN-13: 978-0692394021
ISBN-10: 0692394028

Cover design by Ellen Meyer and Vicki Lesage

*To the three men in my life—the reasons I
love gin quite so much.*

x

INTRODUCTION

Meet Dottie Harris. Dottie spent her late 20s working her way up the career ladder as a project manager. As "one of the boys," Dottie worked hard at the office and played hard out of it.

Whether it was in the pub after work, on sun-drenched holidays, running around in high heels, or even just having movie days with her husband in their immaculately clean house, she lived the self-indulgent life of every childless couple.

Then, when she hit 30, her clock ticked, and she and her husband decided it was time to start a family.

In this modern-day diary, Dottie discovers that as soon as she announces her pregnancy, life as she knows it instantly changes. No more drinking games with the boys, no more energy for the gym and no attention span for the television. Struggling through pregnancy and motherhood, Dottie turns to social networking. She quickly becomes reliant on it—along with gin—using it as a way to reach out to others and come to terms with the funny side of motherhood, whilst realising she's not the only person to consider anything after 7 a.m. a lie in.

Follow her journey as her children grow older, and she gets less enthusiastic.

2007

Dottie Harris HAS REGISTERED AND IS HERE TO JOIN IN THE FUN! DO YOU KNOW Dottie? ADD HER TO YOUR FRIENDS LIST!
November 11, 2007 at 21:15
67 PEOPLE HAVE ADDED Dottie TO THEIR FRIENDS LIST

Dottie Harris is wondering what all this is about then?
November 11, 2007 at 21:27
2 people like this

Dottie Harris is back to the grind.
November 12, 2007 at 7:58
2 people like this

Dottie Harris - Was it 7 p.m. or 8 p.m. tonight guys?
November 12, 2007 at 16:09
2 people like this

Dottie Harris can't wait for a well-earned drink with the team!

November 16, 2007 at 17:25

12 people like this

Dottie Harris is thinking mmmm chips and cheese

November 17, 2007 at 2:59

19 people like this

Dottie Harris is hanging.

November 17, 2007 at 11:23

13 people like this

Dottie Harris has a feeling she's going to be home LATE.

November 20, 2007 at 16:41

16 people like this

Dottie Harris - Tonight? What's the plan?!

November 23, 2007 at 16:46

1 person likes this

Dottie Harris enjoyed Lola's birthday drinks. HAPPY 31st OLD LADY! xxx

November 23, 2007 at 23:46

1 person likes this

Dottie Harris - LOST-athon with nachos and Malteasers and wine.

November 25, 2007 at 14:33

1 person likes this

Dottie Harris is sneaking in a naughty two weeks in Mexico before Christmas. See you on the other side!

December 3, 2007 at 3:27

1 person likes this

Dottie Harris is on her way back from the airport, feeling full and fat, and is now checking her email after not moving from her sun lounger for two weeks.
December 18, 2007 at 23:48
7 people like this

Dottie Harris is back in the office with mince pies and her to-do list.
December 19, 2007 at 8:39
1 person likes this

Dottie Harris is six mince pies down, and they haven't even touched the side. Post-holiday blues?!
December 19, 2007 at 11:57
3 people like this

Dottie Harris totally hasn't just been out on her lunch hour and bought her Christmas party dress!
December 20, 2007 at 13:50
9 people like this

Dottie Harris is in the taxi heading home. Lightweight. :(
December 21, 2007 at 23:55
2 people like this

Dottie Harris does NOT feel good.
December 22, 2007 at 11:37
6 people like this

Dottie Harris can't make tonight. Sorry guys, stomach bug!
December 24, 2007 at 18:22
1 person likes this

Dottie Harris - Merry blooming Christmas from my toilet bowl!

December 25, 2007 at 7:11

12 people like this

Dottie Harris can't believe she's been ill all over Christmas (literally!).

December 26, 2007 at 7:42

3 people like this

Dottie Harris - Another sofa day.

December 27, 2007 at 9:23

13 people like this

Dottie Harris is feeling a bit better. Coco Pops seem to have settled stomach.

December 28, 2007 at 22:51

4 people like this

Dottie Harris is ready for action! Party at ours tomorrow. REMEMBER TO TAKE YOUR SHOES OFF!

December 30, 2007 at 22:43

1 person likes this

Dottie Harris - HAPPY NEW YEAR!!!

December 31, 2007 at 23:58

1 person likes this

2008

Dottie Harris is too tired to be back at work.
January 2, 2008 at 8:31
1 person likes this

Dottie Harris has come home sick AGAIN. :(
January 4, 2008 at 8:31
1 person likes this

Dottie Harris is pregnant. Baby Harris due in JULY!!!
January 11, 2008 at 11:51
18 people like this

Dottie Harris thinks that whoever called it MORNING
sickness is a BIG FAT LIAR.
January 11, 2008 at 16:34
1 person likes this

Dottie Harris is brr!
January 20, 2008 at 10:06
5 people like this

Dottie Harris is heading home to her bed leaving everyone at the pub. Banging head. :(
January 20, 2008 at 21:13
1 person likes this

Dottie Harris is in denial.
January 21, 2008 at 11:34
3 people like this

Dottie Harris is really not up for a night out tonight guys. Sorry, next time I PROMISE. x
January 25, 2008 at 15:12
2 people like this

Dottie Harris is always hungry!
February 12, 2008 at 11:54
3 people like this

Dottie Harris is already unable to do up her work trousers.
February 15, 2008 at 7:23
6 people like this

Dottie Harris wonders if two bumps are normal?!
February 16, 2008 at 9:16
4 people like this

Dottie Harris hearts Yorkshire Puddings.
February 17, 2008 at 17:37
1 person likes this

Dottie Harris would really like to get a proper bump already, rather than just looking like she's eaten all the pie.
February 19, 2008 at 19:31
1 person likes this

Dottie Harris is willing her belly button to pop!
February 23, 2008 at 12:20
1 person likes this

Dottie Harris thinks her shoes may hate her feet.
February 27, 2008 at 18:47
3 people like this

Dottie Harris is watching three men try to put together a sofa. It's not going well.
March 1, 2008 at 17:19
1 person likes this

Dottie Harris wonders how she will manage in the summer if she's this tired now!
March 6, 2008 at 18:45
1 person likes this

Dottie Harris wants brownies.
March 7, 2008 at 21:06
1 person likes this

Dottie Harris thinks the brownies weren't really all that after all.
March 8, 2008 at 9:01
1 person likes this

Dottie Harris is trawling through more than THREE THOUSAND* emails. All from the weekend!

*This may be an exaggeration
March 10, 2008 at 7:36
2 people like this

Dottie Harris wants her birthday present now!!
March 11, 2008 at 9:32
3 people like this

Dottie Harris loves her birthday present!
March 11, 2008 at 22:21
5 people like this

Dottie Harris is grateful for the slow sips of Orange Tango that allowed her to not throw up on her boss during the longest 30-minute meeting in the WORLD.
March 12, 2008 at 15:12
1 person likes this

Dottie Harris thinks the dinner gods are against her. Only Coco Pops appeal and she has none of those in. :(
March 14, 2008 at 20:44
1 person likes this

Dottie Harris has got that Friday feeling. Without the wine though. :(
March 15, 2008 at 18:40
2 people like this

Dottie Harris has replaced the wine with a bottle of Orange Tango and box of Malteasers.
March 15, 2008 at 20:03
5 people like this

Dottie Harris wonders what happened to the whole "eating for two" malarkey. She can't manage a thing!
March 19, 2008 at 23:31
11 people like this

Dottie Harris - McDonald's breakfast followed by Skittles. Perfection.
March 20, 2008 at 9:04
9 people like this

Dottie Harris thinks veto is beginning to sound like a good name.
March 22, 2008 at 19:03
6 people like this

Dottie Harris is building up to THE scan and hoping she doesn't have to keep going out to "empty her bladder just a little bit" this time. Never has she felt more likely to wet herself.
March 28, 2008 at 08:31
11 people like this

Dottie Harris is having a boy!
March 28, 2008 at 15:31
21 people like this

Dottie Harris can't bend.
April 8, 2008 at 15:20
5 people like this

Dottie Harris - Seriously, I still don't have a proper hard bump, and I can't bend. Is this normal?
April 9, 2008 at 11:12
7 people like this

Dottie Harris has approximately four months to find a way to have a baby that doesn't involve giving birth.
April 13, 2008 at 18:06
9 people like this

Dottie Harris has just turned on her out of office and is now in holiday mode!
April 19, 2008 at 19:58
4 people like this

Dottie Harris is on her way to work. :(
April 29, 2008 at 6:36
1 person likes this

Dottie Harris thinks a bowl of Coco Pops would go down a treat right now.
May 4, 2008 at 3:24
1 person likes this

Dottie Harris can't believe Skittles don't come as part of your Bounty Pack.
May 5, 2008 at 9:34
1 person likes this

Dottie Harris is gutted they've gotten rid of the official *Gladiators* theme tune.
May 11, 2008 at 19:42
3 people like this

Dottie Harris can't believe her baby is already the size of A HEAD OF CAULIFLOWER?! I MEAN COME ON!!! *Freaking out*
May 25, 2008 at 11:03
9 people like this

Dottie Harris loves it when people make a loss on *Property Ladder*.
May 28, 2008 at 21:29
2 people like this

Dottie Harris is very happy it's Friday night. She's EXHAUSTED.
May 30, 2008 at 20:12
6 people like this

Dottie Harris has just been told the first baby poo is black. That's not true, is it?
June 5, 2008 at 10:03
5 people like this

Dottie Harris has been to an antenatal class and wishes she could erase the images of THAT video.
June 10, 2008 at 20:22
8 people like this

Dottie Harris has now ordered her pram :D
June 11, 2008 at 19:34
11 people like this

Dottie Harris is so so tired.
June 12, 2008 at 7:35
1 person likes this

Dottie Harris is fed up with being fat.
June 14, 2008 at 13:57
3 people like this

Dottie Harris has 24 working days left.
June 15, 2008 at 14:11
5 people like this

Dottie Harris has 23.5 working days left.
June 16, 2008 at 12:46
6 people like this

Dottie Harris has 23 working days left.
June 16, 2008 at 17:17
2 people like this

Dottie Harris has 22.5 working days left.
June 17, 2008 at 10:57
3 people like this

Dottie Harris has 22 working days left.
June 17, 2008 at 16:26
1 person likes this

Dottie Harris has 20 working days left.
June 19, 2008 at 19:20
1 person likes this

Dottie Harris thinks Gaviscon is the future.
June 21, 2008 at 17:53
9 people like this

Dottie Harris has 18.5 working days left.
June 23, 2008 at 11:14
3 people like this

Dottie Harris has 18 working days left!
June 23, 2008 at 17:28
5 people like this

Dottie Harris has 17 working days left. Suddenly that's
not enough!!
June 24, 2008 at 18:34
7 people like this

Dottie Harris has just held a newborn vest over her bump. There is NO WAY that is coming out of her.
June 26, 2008 at 7:32
1 person likes this

Dottie Harris thinks swollen fingers are the new black.
June 30, 2008 at 7:32
4 people like this

Dottie Harris is hot and grumpo.
July 1, 2008 at 16:40
1 person likes this

Dottie Harris is a "lady wot lunches."
July 4, 2008 at 18:21
1 person likes this

Dottie Harris has put the book describing giving birth in the freezer.
July 8, 2008 at 23:47
4 people like this

Dottie Harris is a cleaning machine. A slightly slow and broken cleaning machine!
July 9, 2008 at 8:27
4 people like this

Dottie Harris is fat.
July 12, 2008 at 12:39
1 person likes this

Dottie Harris thinks that stomping her feet and kicking a bollard perhaps wasn't the most dignified response to the chip shop being closed (but it had nothing to do with hormones).

July 14, 2008 at 20:35

9 people like this

Dottie Harris thinks her husband is a mean boy who is just being mean.

July 20, 2008 at 8:27

3 people like this

Dottie Harris thinks that's enough kicking now, please baby!

July 23, 2008 at 8:46

1 person likes this

Dottie Harris should stop counting down the days.

July 24, 2008 at 14:59

1 person likes this

Dottie Harris has just seen a child tantruming in Waitrose. She's changed her mind.

July 24, 2008 at 17:59

7 people like this

Dottie Harris hearts her hammock and the sun. Now, about that gin? Oh. :(

July 25, 2008 at 10:38

9 people like this

Dottie Harris thinks she's stuck in her hammock…

July 25, 2008 at 10:50

7 people like this

Dottie Harris … er help?!
July 25, 2008 at 11:15
12 people like this

Dottie Harris wonders why she's chosen today to tidy out her handbags?
July 27, 2008 at 10:06
5 people like this

Dottie Harris - DUE DATE!!!!!!!!!!
July 28, 2008 at 7:01
5 people like this

Dottie Harris = fed up.
July 29, 2008 at 8:49
3 people like this

Dottie Harris is aiming to be a Desperate Housewife.
July 30, 2008 at 11:07
2 people like this

Dottie Harris - Seriously kid? HURRY UP!!!
August 4, 2008 at 13:23
9 people like this

Dottie Harris is a little grumpy about being tired and achy all the time.
August 5, 2008 at 9:57
2 people like this

Dottie Harris has finally braved a proper profile picture. Must be the hormones!
August 5, 2008 at 17:23
10 people like this

Dottie Harris is going to invent something Dragon's Den-worthy... You see if she doesn't!
August 6, 2008 at 18:44
2 people like this

Dottie Harris is a mummy!
August 7, 2008 at 13:42
23 people like this

Dottie Harris can't stop looking at the little angel she's created <3
August 8, 2008 at 3:19
19 people like this

Dottie Harris never realised just how BLACK poo could be, or just how dangerous breast milk is, especially when it sprays your partner in the eye.
August 12, 2008 at 15:50
11 people like this

Dottie Harris has never experienced such a loud cry.
August 13, 2008 at 20:50
3 people like this

Dottie Harris has definitely changed her mind.
August 13, 2008 at 23:36
6 people like this

Dottie Harris was never told about the "not being put down and feeding every hour" bit.
August 23, 2008 at 15:50
4 people like this

Dottie Harris wonders if anybody wants a baby?
August 24, 2008 at 22:30
8 people like this

Dottie Harris could do with a couple of hours sleep.
August 31, 2008 at 3:12
3 people like this

Dottie Harris is a pram-pushing machine.
September 1, 2008 at 4:35
4 people like this

Dottie Harris has been a mummy for an ENTIRE
MONTH!!!
September 7, 2008 at 13:10
14 people like this

Dottie Harris might not give the baby away now.
September 11, 2008 at 8:35
9 people like this

Dottie Harris would like to thank whoever invented the
baby sling.
September 12, 2008 at 2:40
4 people like this

Dottie Harris didn't realise how far baby poo can shoot
downwards.
September 12, 2008 at 11:10
8 people like this

Dottie Harris has discovered that using baby wipes is
easier than changing your jeans.
September 18, 2008 at 9:30
4 people like this

Dottie Harris loves that her baby boy loves when she
sings to Leona Lewis. Shame nobody else does.
September 23, 2008 at 18:41
3 people like this

Dottie Harris has never witnessed a perfect "wee arc" before, especially not at 3 a.m.
September 29, 2008 at 3:23
9 people like this

Dottie Harris is going to try putting her boy to bed awake.
October 1, 2008 at 18:55
3 people like this

Dottie Harris is currently bouncing a screaming child in the dark.
October 1, 2008 at 19:35
4 people like this

Dottie Harris thinks that didn't go as well as anticipated.
October 1, 2008 at 20:25
5 people like this

Dottie Harris wonders how sleeping babies know when you sit down.
October 2, 2008 at 21:05
11 people like this

Dottie Harris HAS WALKED OUT OF HER SON'S ROOM AND HE DIDN'T SCREAM!!!!
October 14, 2008 at 19:05
9 people like this

Dottie Harris has only just now noticed the sick down the back of her top. How long has that been there?
October 20, 2008 at 16:24
5 people like this

Dottie Harris has a squidgy little pumpkin to share the Haribo with.
October 31, 2008 at 17:59
3 people like this

Dottie Harris is becoming a dab hand at eating all her meals with one hand (and usually one boob on display).
November 2, 2008 at 12:45
14 people like this

Dottie Harris can't get over how much little boy smiles melt her heart.
November 5, 2008 at 10:24
20 people like this

Dottie Harris sometimes really wishes her son wouldn't treat a bottle or a dummy like something from the devil.
November 10, 2008 at 21:46
2 people like this

Dottie Harris - Seriously, is it normal for babies to reject the dummy so angrily?
November 11, 2008 at 2:41
2 people like this

Dottie Harris finds the rain cover on the pram a tad frustrating, especially when it gets steamed up.
November 15, 2008 at 14:05
20 people like this

Dottie Harris has knelt in poo and been wee'd on TWICE and it's not even 9 a.m.
November 21, 2008 at 7:15
3 people like this

Dottie Harris is going on a date with her husband
WITHOUT THE BABY.
November 25, 2008 at 19:59
9 people like this

Dottie Harris has come to terms with the fact she gave
birth to a baby monster.
November 27, 2008 at 7:01
13 people like this

Dottie Harris thinks it's amazing that a man cold is worse
than a woman cold!
November 28, 2008 at 8:41
16 people like this

Dottie Harris wishes she could slightly hang her bum out
of shorts like Britney Spears just did on *The X Factor*!
November 30, 2008 at 18:55
1 person likes this

Dottie Harris is still in bed!
December 3, 2008 at 8:16
7 people like this

Dottie Harris is fed up with chapped lips! Damn you
winter wind!
December 3, 2008 at 18:39
1 person likes this

Dottie Harris has been married for 5 years and 5 hours. x
December 6, 2008 at 20:50
12 people like this

Dottie Harris has a feeling The Monster may not be as excited about homemade apple puree as she is!
December 7, 2008 at 10:13
9 people like this

Dottie Harris wishes she'd not bought biscuits.
December 9, 2008 at 11:37
6 people like this

Dottie Harris wants gin.
December 11, 2008 at 7:42
3 people like this

Dottie Harris is excited about getting The Monster's first Christmas tree!
December 13, 2008 at 13:32
13 people like this

Dottie Harris is going to win the next *X Factor*. FACT.
December 13, 2008 at 22:51
4 people like this

Dottie Harris is thinking pancakes.
December 19, 2008 at 9:19
1 person likes this

Dottie Harris is ready for a large gin and tonic.
December 20, 2008 at 18:30
1 person likes this

Dottie Harris can't believe her oven is broken.
December 21, 2008 at 18:48
5 people like this

Dottie Harris is a happy Mummy!
December 23, 2008 at 9:07
6 people like this

Dottie Harris is looking forward to mulled wine and mince pies!
December 24, 2008 at 16:05
3 people like this

Dottie Harris is pleased Santa said she could have the glass of port and mince pie The Monster left out for him!
December 24, 2008 at 23:44
9 people like this

Dottie Harris is so cold she thinks her feet might fall off.
December 27, 2008 at 21:32
3 people like this

Dottie Harris has lost the will to live. In The Night Garden on re-run can break ANYONE'S brain.
December 28, 2008 at 16:03
1 person likes this

Dottie Harris is seeing the New Year in with the two boys in her life. Have a good one everyone. Here's to 2009 and getting some sleep. x
December 31, 2008 at 23:45
23 people like this

2009

Dottie Harris has officially become one of those mums who picks her child's nose and doesn't even flinch.
January 1, 2009 at 14:36
11 people like this

Dottie Harris thinks the diet isn't going well. Darn those Christmas biscuits!
January 3, 2009 at 13:12
3 people like this

Dottie Harris is bloody cold!
January 5, 2009 at 7:12
2 people like this

Dottie Harris feels like the most horrid Mummy in the world. The Monster is NOT impressed with the bottle. :(
January 6, 2009 at 19:28
7 people like this

Dottie Harris has coffee for the first time in more than a year! Ahh lovely!
January 8, 2009 at 8:29
3 people like this

Dottie Harris LOVES Mr. Motivator!
January 16, 2009 at 8:32
3 people like this

Dottie Harris is a changed person. She's packing light. Well, thinking about it anyway!
January 16, 2009 at 20:19
6 people like this

Dottie Harris is carrying a little holiday weight. :(
January 23, 2009 at 8:30
2 people like this

Dottie Harris got rid of all the Hobnobs today. She was only doing it for the good of her belly.
January 23, 2009 at 19:06
9 people like this

Dottie Harris has cooking wine.
January 23, 2009 at 19:18
7 people like this

Dottie Harris has a headache.
January 24, 2009 at 16:19
2 people like this

Dottie Harris is pleased her little headache has finally gone (to bed).
January 24, 2009 at 19:08
3 people like this

Dottie Harris is trying to ignore the ironing.
January 28, 2009 at 9:58
4 people like this

Dottie Harris wonders how to explain to her son that sucking the edge of the table isn't cool?!
Throws up a bit in mouth
January 29, 2009 at 15:28
9 people like this

Dottie Harris is still in bed!
January 30, 2009 at 8:21
2 people like this

Dottie Harris is still in her dressing gown and feeling lazy!
February 2, 2009 at 9:45
3 people like this

Dottie Harris has a poorly little boy. :(
February 4, 2009 at 8:15
2 people like this

Dottie Harris can't believe the televisions in the children's ward switch off after 9 p.m. What's she gonna do all night?!
February 4, 2009 at 21:39
7 people like this

Dottie Harris is tired but on her way home with her baby boy.
February 5, 2009 at 9:50
3 people like this

Dottie Harris is thinking the bug she caught from The Monster isn't so bad. After all she's lost 3 lbs in 24 hours. Hurrah!
February 7, 2009 at 18:32
4 people like this

Dottie Harris is pondering whether to have gin or wine. Or both?
February 9, 2009 at 18:56
7 people like this

Dottie Harris is happy to notice a bit of back flab on Rihanna in her latest video.
February 10, 2009 at 17:02
3 people like this

Dottie Harris is wondering why she's bothering to drink caffeine-free Diet Coke. What's the point?
February 11, 2009 at 14:57
1 person likes this

Dottie Harris is totally intending to marry Phil from Phil and Kirstie.
February 11, 2009 at 21:03
3 people like this

Dottie Harris had forgotten what a kitchen goddess she actually is!
February 14, 2009 at 19:34
3 people like this

Dottie Harris is grumpily picking pine needles out of the lounge carpet (STILL).
February 15, 2009 at 19:02
4 people like this

Dottie Harris cannot believe the boy slept through but she didn't!
February 18, 2009 at 8:43
3 people like this

Dottie Harris is wistfully thinking how amazing it would have been to be Jennifer Grey in *Dirty Dancing*.
February 20, 2009 at 20:11
8 people like this

Dottie Harris is feeling fat from her homemade chicken jalfrezi and is now drinking wine and considering ice cream. Oh yes.
February 21, 2009 at 21:31
1 person likes this

Dottie Harris is not loving today's wake up time courtesy of The Monster.
February 22, 2009 at 5:31
1 person likes this

Dottie Harris is thinking gin & tonic practically counts as water. It's clear, isn't it?!
February 23, 2009 at 19:32
3 people like this

Dottie Harris is drowning in wine.
February 28, 2009 at 19:53
5 people like this

Dottie Harris is wondering where she can buy a Calpol drip from. Hang the expense!
March 2, 2009 at 8:49
7 people like this

Dottie Harris thinks teaching the boy to crawl after a can of Diet Coke could backfire if it works!
March 2, 2009 at 17:04
4 people like this

Dottie Harris was going to leave mopping the floor until tomorrow, then she noticed a small child licking it.
March 3, 2009 at 14:45
2 people like this

Dottie Harris has chocolate eater's remorse.
March 4, 2009 at 14:55
3 people like this

Dottie Harris is not broody! Nope. Not at all.
March 5, 2009 at 22:08
3 people like this

Dottie Harris is wondering why you always think "one last gin" when you get home is a good idea?
March 6, 2009 at 8:48
1 person likes this

Dottie Harris is not happy she's getting close to her birthday.
March 7, 2009 at 20:01
1 person likes this

Dottie Harris is one year older. Yay.
March 11, 2009 at 20:01
23 people like this

Dottie Harris is a bit chilly, but loving that everything in the garden is starting to bud up!
March 19, 2009 at 15:26
3 people like this

Dottie Harris was going to have a bath and a glass of wine later, but the new NEXT catalogue is now here. That takes priority.
March 19, 2009 at 17:22
1 person likes this

Dottie Harris thinks her son is very clever for making her breakfast in bed this morning!
March 22, 2009 at 19:08
1 person likes this

Dottie Harris is trying to explain to her son that 6 a.m. is not the new black.
March 24, 2009 at 7:55
3 people like this

Dottie Harris is thinking her fake tan may not have gone exactly to plan.
March 24, 2009 at 20:20
4 people like this

Dottie Harris is ready for the gym. Size 0 here she comes!
March 29, 2009 at 8:44
2 people like this

Dottie Harris thinks she'll pass on the gym today.
March 30, 2009 at 9:50
2 people like this

Dottie Harris is a changed person. Rice cake is ground into the carpet, and she almost doesn't care. ALMOST.
March 31, 2009 at 13:53
8 people like this

Dottie Harris is happy in the sunshine! Front path weeded, windows open... now to fix the front door seal that the boy managed to pull out!

April 1, 2009 at 9:36

3 people like this

Dottie Harris ran to the gym, worked out, ran back and is now deciding which rock to die under.

April 4, 2009 at 9:51

2 people like this

Dottie Harris thinks her legs might fall off.

April 4, 2009 at 19:11

3 people like this

Dottie Harris thinks she may love her new Dustbuster more than diamonds.

April 5, 2009 at 17:32

1 person likes this

Dottie Harris cannot believe there is no wine in the house at all. Oh well, gin it is!

April 11, 2009 at 17:55

1 person likes this

Dottie Harris has been pretending to be the Flake girl. But with a Creme Egg. And not flooding the bathroom. After all, that would be a mess to clean up.

April 12, 2009 at 19:26

5 people like this

Dottie Harris feels she may be a rather horrid person for putting cat food on the sprinkler then turning it on.

April 14, 2009 at 10:03

8 people like this

Dottie Harris has done a very Monica-esque thing and hoovered her Dustbuster and Dustbusted her hoover.
April 14, 2009 at 14:50
3 people like this

Dottie Harris is loving the fact that her baby says "Mama" and then gives her a kiss and doesn't believe it's just a coincidence AT ALL. OK?
April 29, 2009 at 17:15
6 people like this

Dottie Harris is thinking the Special K diet isn't going well. She's not had any this week.
May 1, 2009 at 18:12
1 person likes this

Dottie Harris thinks her son hunts out danger.
May 2, 2009 at 17:18
3 people like this

Dottie Harris is concerned. She may have to wash up the pots in her dishwasher if the third time she sets it going it doesn't work!!
May 3, 2009 at 7:59
3 people like this

Dottie Harris is not thinking about the smiley-faced potatoes in the freezer.
May 5, 2009 at 9:51
1 person likes this

Dottie Harris doesn't need to worry about the smiley faces in the freezer as they are no longer there.
May 5, 2009 at 18:49
2 people like this

Dottie Harris is waiting to see what The Monster thinks is more dangerous: the door stop or the stair gate?!
May 6, 2009 at 10:53
3 people like this

Dottie Harris is wishing she'd not put her skinny jeans in the tumble dryer.
May 7, 2009 at 8:09
1 person likes this

Dottie Harris is wondering if there will ever be a day again where her washing machine isn't going?!
May 7, 2009 at 14:01
2 people like this

Dottie Harris is slightly more excited than she should be about using her new plates tonight.
May 12, 2009 at 18:26
1 person likes this

Dottie Harris appears to be struggling more with the baby-proofed cupboards than The Monster does.
May 16, 2009 at 18:19
1 person likes this

Dottie Harris has just had a mass bikini trying on session and is pleased to say she may be allowed to eat before she goes away!
May 17, 2009 at 19:06
4 people like this

Dottie Harris has jam in her hair and small child sick on her fridge. It's a glam life.
May 20, 2009 at 16:03
7 people like this

Dottie Harris is wondering how her son knows how to change the brightness on the TV but she doesn't.
May 20, 2009 at 16:13
9 people like this

Dottie Harris is looking forward to picking up The Monster's new car seat after he escaped from his current one on the way home from town yesterday.
May 23, 2009 at 6:35
2 people like this

Dottie Harris is going to make sangria.
May 23, 2009 at 11:31
2 people like this

Dottie Harris thinks she may have drunk the entire world's supply of alcohol last night.
May 24, 2009 at 6:29
3 people like this

Dottie Harris wonders why she was stupid enough to think emptying the cupboards of naughty things would stop her from being hungry. Instead she is STARVING to DEATH.
May 26, 2009 at 13:58
1 person likes this

Dottie Harris can't do it! She just can't pack light!
May 27, 2009 at 11:47
5 people like this

Dottie Harris is baffled. Why do *The Apprentice* contestants ALWAYS leave their ironing until they only have half an hour before the cars get there?!
May 27, 2009 at 20:23
3 people like this

Dottie Harris thinks 15 kg of luggage per person is ridiculous.
May 29, 2009 at 9:49
3 people like this

Dottie Harris is switching off from reality... now!
May 30, 2009 at 4:55
9 people like this

Dottie Harris is back in the blinkin' UK.
June 6, 2009 at 19:00
1 person likes this

Dottie Harris is trying to ignore the fact that each room in her house seems to have exploded into a big pile of tidying up.
June 9, 2009 at 11:05
1 person likes this

Dottie Harris wishes she could find the jelly The Monster threw across the room during a tantrum at teatime. :(
June 10, 2009 at 17:12
9 people like this

Dottie Harris can't believe Zack Morris is back!
June 10, 2009 at 20:25
3 people like this

Dottie Harris is very proud that both she and The Monster made it through his first morning at nursery school unscathed!
June 16, 2009 at 17:27
6 people like this

Dottie Harris is wondering if she can trade her son in for an Alfa Romeo Mito in black?
June 17, 2009 at 17:09
2 people like this

Dottie Harris is mega excited to see the results of the carpet cleaner she's just put on in the lounge!
June 18, 2009 at 13:35
2 people like this

Dottie Harris doesn't think the carpet cleaner worked. She also can't quite believe she used the phrase "mega excited."
June 18, 2009 at 16:18
1 person likes this

Dottie Harris thinks there should be a drive-thru Starbucks.
June 23, 2009 at 7:36
3 people like this

Dottie Harris is watching The Monster eat the hose pipe. Would it be wrong to turn it on?
June 24, 2009 at 13:09
6 people like this

Dottie Harris thinks it's time for another cup of tea!
June 25, 2009 at 8:06
2 people like this

Dottie Harris is missing her boy more than she thought she would!
June 25, 2009 at 11:18
7 people like this

Dottie Harris feels a bit thick. She just fell off her chair. Thank God nobody else was here to see!

June 25, 2009 at 16:08

3 people like this

Dottie Harris is excited as she has a bottle of pink gin on the counter waiting for tonight!

June 26, 2009 at 15:46

2 people like this

Dottie Harris is attempting to make a homemade iced coffee.

June 30, 2009 at 8:59

1 person likes this

Dottie Harris failed with the iced coffee so is hitting the (pink) gin instead. x

June 30, 2009 at 18:10

2 people like this

Dottie Harris thinks the child on the Glade Touch & Fresh advert makes her more angry than a child should!

July 6, 2009 at 15:07

3 people like this

Dottie Harris is wondering why the young lads in JLS (yes young) insist on touching their "area" in their new music video. Kids today!

July 7, 2009 at 7:33

11 people like this

Dottie Harris thinks the baby food diet that all the stars are going on about doesn't necessarily mean finishing off fishcake, mash and beans.

July 8, 2009 at 11:51

3 people like this

Dottie Harris is wondering if it's worth gluing the blind shut so The Monster stops opening it at nap time.
July 9, 2009 at 9:59
5 people like this

Dottie Harris is feeling quite holy. Instead of throwing herself at the mercy of Pizza Hut as she walked past it, she settled for a Caramel Light Frappuccino from Starbucks.
July 12, 2009 at 12:49
2 people like this

Dottie Harris is looking forward to The Monster being in bed so she can indulge in a pink gin and some trashy television. :)
July 12, 2009 at 17:45
2 people like this

Dottie Harris loves Tim Gunn.
July 13, 2009 at 11:03
4 people like this

Dottie Harris is wondering why she bothers mopping the floor when she has a husband and son.
July 15, 2009 at 12:44
3 people like this

Dottie Harris thinks drinking during the day may be the only way to go.
July 15, 2009 at 15:55
5 people like this

Dottie Harris is slightly concerned that the scales are going in the wrong direction.
July 18, 2009 at 7:59
2 people like this

Dottie Harris has tried to hide the ironing behind the chair in the lounge. It doesn't bode well that the pile is poking out of the top.

July 19, 2009 at 9:25

1 person likes this

Dottie Harris thinks the narrator from In The Night Garden is just out to cause trouble!

July 19, 2009 at 17:09

1 person likes this

Dottie Harris is getting ready to go SHOPPING!

July 20, 2009 at 9:39

2 people like this

Dottie Harris wonders if she went to sleep in July and woke up in October?! SO COLD!

July 21, 2009 at 18:33

1 person likes this

Dottie Harris has just caught her son about to fish breadsticks out of the bin! Thank goodness he didn't get to eat them!

July 22, 2009 at 16:11

3 people like this

Dottie Harris is opening the wine.

July 22, 2009 at 19:13

7 people like this

Dottie Harris is tackling a mound of clothes. She WILL have a capsule wardrobe!

July 23, 2009 at 14:12

3 people like this

Dottie Harris is covered in amoxicillin, baby snot and baby phlegm. :(
July 24, 2009 at 17:38
5 people like this

Dottie Harris is thinking she shouldn't have cut tea out of her diet this weekend.
July 25, 2009 at 9:17
3 people like this

Dottie Harris is enjoying the freedom of having all of the stair gates open!
July 28, 2009 at 7:29
5 people like this

Dottie Harris is no longer enjoying her son's game of crawling up to her and yanking her jeans down!
July 28, 2009 at 16:48
9 people like this

Dottie Harris is having a test run with The Monster's birthday cake. She is now sitting and watching her oven for 23 minutes.
July 30, 2009 at 15:09
1 person likes this

Dottie Harris thinks it's not gone well.
July 30, 2009 at 16:09
1 person likes this

Dottie Harris is dusting off her big wine glass, which means TECHNICALLY she is only having one glass of red.
August 1, 2009 at 18:26
3 people like this

Dottie Harris is witnessing a mega tantrum all because she wouldn't let her son steal her pen.
August 3, 2009 at 17:25
3 people like this

Dottie Harris is cleaning before the potential cleaner shows up.
August 4, 2009 at 8:46
7 people like this

Dottie Harris is thinking now would be a good time to instill "it's the thought that counts" in her son. That or pop to M&S to buy a cake and lie about it.
August 5, 2009 at 17:42
1 person likes this

Dottie Harris has a 1-year-old! Happy 1st birthday to my boy! x
August 7, 2009 at 7:26
26 people like this

Dottie Harris thinks she may have over-celebrated at The Monster's birthday party and is now paying the price. :(
August 9, 2009 at 6:37
4 people like this

Dottie Harris has just had to give all of her quiche to her son. How many times: DOTTIE DOESN'T SHARE FOOD!!!!!!!!!!!!
August 10, 2009 at 12:36
7 people like this

Dottie Harris thinks her son is on a fine line!
August 10, 2009 at 17:14
3 people like this

Dottie Harris has overslept. Never rely on child as an alarm clock!
August 11, 2009 at 7:33
2 people like this

Dottie Harris really wishes she hadn't eaten so many Oreos today.
August 11, 2009 at 14:56
1 person likes this

Dottie Harris is ready for a gin and tonic and a hot bath!
August 12, 2009 at 16:58
3 people like this

Dottie Harris has another Monster-free day, and is looking forward to visiting NEXT without the risk of chocolate milk being flicked at the clothes.
August 13, 2009 at 7:50
5 people like this

Dottie Harris is having trouble understanding how her cupboards are full yet there is NO FOOD IN THERE!
August 13, 2009 at 11:27
3 people like this

Dottie Harris is looking at the sky thinking it's going to rain on her newly put out laundry. :(
August 14, 2009 at 9:07
2 people like this

Dottie Harris is thinking her next car should be a BMW X3. Apparently then you own the road and can drive like a knob.
August 15, 2009 at 18:16
8 people like this

Dottie Harris is wondering whether after closing her eyes and counting to 10 all the ironing will be done?!
August 17, 2009 at 12:05
1 person likes this

Dottie Harris has a small child for sale.
August 17, 2009 at 14:54
5 people like this

Dottie Harris is on the train. The first one. Two more to go until she reaches her destination!
August 19, 2009 at 6:54
5 people like this

Dottie Harris is on her way home! x
August 19, 2009 at 17:57
3 people like this

Dottie Harris has just been told there is wine, curry, pops & naan at home waiting for her!
August 19, 2009 at 18:18
6 people like this

Dottie Harris is thinking this rain is going to ruin her hair! :(
August 20, 2009 at 10:09
3 people like this

Dottie Harris is wishing the spider that lives in her wing mirror would stop scuttling out and staring at her every time she opens the car window.
August 21, 2009 at 10:00
11 people like this

Dottie Harris is deciding whether to order her CDs alphabetically or by genre.
August 24, 2009 at 10:59
4 people like this

Dottie Harris is starting to panic about getting up and out of the house 5 days a week. Day 2 of practice and they all overslept!
August 25, 2009 at 7:33
1 person likes this

Dottie Harris has a spider holding her hostage in the study. Is it the one that lives in her car?!
August 25, 2009 at 10:23
3 people like this

Dottie Harris is contemplating going back to bed for another nap before officially getting up.
August 28, 2009 at 7:13
7 people like this

Dottie Harris is really beginning to worry about the spider stalking situation.
August 29, 2009 at 14:36
7 people like this

Dottie Harris is on her last day of freedom! EEP!
September 1, 2009 at 7:18
3 people like this

Dottie Harris survived and luckily remembered how to walk in high heels!
September 2, 2009 at 7:18
9 people like this

Dottie Harris can't believe she made it until the end of the week. She needs an early night now!
September 4, 2009 at 17:46
3 people like this

Dottie Harris has finally topped up her pink gin supply. x
September 5, 2009 at 15:25
2 people like this

Dottie Harris must not dip her Twirl into her morning cup of coffee.
September 7, 2009 at 8:36
3 people like this

Dottie Harris is not going to use the vending machine today.
September 9, 2009 at 11:04
1 person likes this

Dottie Harris didn't use the vending machine but is ordering pizza.
September 9, 2009 at 19:19
3 people like this

Dottie Harris ate a whole bag of Skittles to give herself energy but feels sick now.
September 10, 2009 at 10:48
2 people like this

Dottie Harris can't believe she set fire to her oven gloves. :(
September 12, 2009 at 20:38
3 people like this

Dottie Harris thinks she may be a little unfit!
September 16, 2009 at 9:45
4 people like this

Dottie Harris hates high heels but couldn't live without them.
September 16, 2009 at 17:07
8 people like this

Dottie Harris is on the train home and has just seen somebody add COKE to their gin! FOOL!
September 16, 2009 at 17:25
11 people like this

Dottie Harris doesn't care that it's only September. The heating is going ON!
September 17, 2009 at 9:41
1 person likes this

Dottie Harris has brain ache. :(
September 17, 2009 at 16:19
1 person likes this

Dottie Harris thinks she collected the devil child from nursery school.
September 17, 2009 at 18:31
3 people like this

Dottie Harris has a huge coffee stain on her lovely shirt, so is using the train Wi-Fi to do some retail therapy.
September 18, 2009 at 15:02
3 people like this

Dottie Harris is feeling very guilty that her baby is poorly while she's stuck on a train and can't get to him. :(
September 18, 2009 at 15:48
1 person likes this

Dottie Harris has a feeling she's going to drink a lot of gin tonight.
September 19, 2009 at 16:40
2 people like this

Dottie Harris feels like she has a newborn again. Needs sleep.
September 20, 2009 at 9:03
3 people like this

Dottie Harris thinks she may actually be a zombie.
September 21, 2009 at 14:23
6 people like this

Dottie Harris is feeling less like a zombie but has a mega sore throat and is hoping she's not caught the man flu. After all it's the worst illness in the world!
September 22, 2009 at 7:08
6 people like this

Dottie Harris Chips. Wine. Trash. Sleep.
September 23, 2009 at 19:50
4 people like this

Dottie Harris is on her way to a meeting but smells of toddler sick. Classy.
September 24, 2009 at 6:56
9 people like this

Dottie Harris is thinking it would be a very bad idea for her to fall asleep on the train.
September 24, 2009 at 17:29
3 people like this

Dottie Harris has had lots of sick and hardly any food all weekend but has lost no weight. How unfair.
September 27, 2009 at 19:18
3 people like this

Dottie Harris has her huge wine glass at the ready!
October 5, 2009 at 19:10
1 person likes this

Dottie Harris has been in the car for almost two hours.
October 6, 2009 at 7:46
3 people like this

Dottie Harris hates traffic, the A1 and the cold. She also *may* have resorted to eating the sandwich that was meant for lunch.
October 6, 2009 at 8:21
1 person likes this

Dottie Harris may have a full-blown tantrum at what will end up being a 5, maybe 6, hour commute!
October 6, 2009 at 10:34
3 people like this

Dottie Harris made it to work in five hours!
October 6, 2009 at 11:03
5 people like this

Dottie Harris can't believe just how much she loves her son right now.

October 7, 2009 at 19:49

8 people like this

Dottie Harris doesn't understand how her house gets so untidy and always needs cleaning when she is hardly ever there!

October 10, 2009 at 9:49

1 person likes this

Dottie Harris is hoping her itchy eyes are tired and not conjunctivitis caught from the boy. Wine should cure it.

October 15, 2009 at 18:15

1 person likes this

Dottie Harris just got asked for ID when buying beer. Good times.

October 17, 2009 at 16:12

3 people like this

Dottie Harris has just painted her son's toenails in the vain hope he'll leave her alone for half an hour.

October 18, 2009 at 11:21

5 people like this

Dottie Harris is DYING. Stupid flu.

October 18, 2009 at 23:46

3 people like this

Dottie Harris is still unwell but maybe not dying after all.

October 20, 2009 at 9:00

1 person likes this

Dottie Harris has pizza on the way, which is making her less grumpy (but only slightly).
October 20, 2009 at 19:05
2 people like this

Dottie Harris had a 9 a.m. lie in and is making the family pancakes!
October 24, 2009 at 9:15
1 person likes this

Dottie Harris is on her way to IKEA to buy lots of stuff for The Monster's playroom!
October 24, 2009 at 11:04
3 people like this

Dottie Harris must be ill. She has spent a fortune at IKEA but didn't get anything for herself!
October 24, 2009 at 15:12
1 person likes this

Dottie Harris is going to London to buy Heat Magazine (and go to meetings, but Heat Magazine is the priority).
October 27, 2009 at 20:01
3 people like this

Dottie Harris is wishing she hadn't picked the nail varnish off her finger nail as now her hands look skanky.
October 30, 2009 at 12:34
2 people like this

Dottie Harris has a curry on, the cooking wine poured and the doorbell off.
October 31, 2009 at 19:48
1 person likes this

Dottie Harris thinks based on Jedward she may actually win *The X Factor* next year.
October 31, 2009 at 21:29
6 people like this

Dottie Harris has a small child for sale.
November 5, 2009 at 18:33
2 people like this

Dottie Harris believes maybe she's too involved in work after referring to her son as "Email."
November 6, 2009 at 17:38
1 person likes this

Dottie Harris thinks it's time to find a long lost relative that dies suddenly and leaves her lots of money!
November 8, 2009 at 18:01
4 people like this

Dottie Harris can't believe her husband is so selfish that he doesn't want to get 2 for 1 Tuesday Domino's. She's going to ask him if he thinks she's fat.
November 10, 2009 at 17:37
3 people like this

Dottie Harris wonders why she spends so much time avoiding something she needs to do before she logs off.
November 13, 2009 at 18:13
2 people like this

Dottie Harris has a feeling it's going to be a long night based on sobbing child. :(
November 15, 2009 at 22:47
1 person likes this

Dottie Harris can't believe the amount of snot and phlegm that comes out of her little man.
November 17, 2009 at 9:38
2 people like this

Dottie Harris had another bad night with the poorly Monster (notice how the sympathy is starting to disappear?).
November 18, 2009 at 9:55
4 people like this

Dottie Harris is pleased The Monster is sleeping again.
November 20, 2009 at 8:25
11 people like this

Dottie Harris can smell a smell she doesn't want to smell.
November 21, 2009 at 6:55
2 people like this

Dottie Harris can't believe what she's smelling AGAIN.
November 22, 2009 at 6:43
1 person likes this

Dottie Harris just tried to climb over the stair gate. BIG mistake.
November 24, 2009 at 19:51
7 people like this

Dottie Harris has crossed 90% of things off her to-do list today. Time for a gin to celebrate.
November 25, 2009 at 19:55
4 people like this

Dottie Harris totally didn't just get water into her son's eyes as karma for the tantrum leaving nursery school earlier.
November 27, 2009 at 18:26
13 people like this

Dottie Harris is on a date (with her husband, don't panic)!
November 28, 2009 at 19:51
2 people like this

Dottie Harris is a very cheap (and sleepy) date.
November 28, 2009 at 21:35
5 people like this

Dottie Harris can't believe her husband bought The Monster an Advent calendar this year but not her. How things change.
December 1, 2009 at 7:19
9 people like this

Dottie Harris has just dropped the boy off and is getting ready to celebrate her wedding anniversary a day early. x
December 5, 2009 at 17:19
4 people like this

Dottie Harris has decided she's going to hide at home forever and ever amen.
December 9, 2009 at 16:28
1 person likes this

Dottie Harris wonders how her email inbox keeps filling up quicker than she can respond to them. LEAVE ME ALONE!!!!!!!
December 10, 2009 at 17:32
1 person likes this

Dottie Harris is at her mum's with a glass of wine. Bliss!
December 11, 2009 at 19:52
2 people like this

Dottie Harris has got the tree and is ready to trim up!
December 13, 2009 at 11:01
2 people like this

Dottie Harris really doesn't like it when her family helps her decorate the tree.
December 13, 2009 at 12:05
2 people like this

Dottie Harris is pleased her son likes putting things away in their proper place and is hoping he'll also like washing and cleaning.
December 15, 2009 at 7:59
5 people like this

Dottie Harris is convinced she lives on an Indian burial ground.
December 16, 2009 at 21:29
7 people like this

Dottie Harris is trying to decide if her son should be a pudding or an elf this Christmas?
December 17, 2009 at 20:58
3 people like this

Dottie Harris has just discovered a pool of sick in the toy box. Nice.
December 19, 2009 at 10:17
11 people like this

Dottie Harris has just found a load of laundry behind the freezer. :(

December 20, 2009 at 8:11

3 people like this

Dottie Harris is thinking death by email.

December 23, 2009 at 13:28

2 people like this

Dottie Harris could really do with signing off for Christmas please.

December 23, 2009 at 21:05

1 person likes this

Dottie Harris is officially signed off, and intends to get drunk now (in the next 10 mins before she falls asleep on the sofa).

December 23, 2009 at 22:09

3 people like this

Dottie Harris loves Christmas morning with a toddler. Have a wicked one, everybody! x

December 25, 2009 at 8:13

12 people like this

Dottie Harris is thinking somebody has been giving the boy coffee! He hasn't stopped in 3 days!

December 27, 2009 at 9:33

2 people like this

Dottie Harris is wondering if it's too early for a G&T?

December 28, 2009 at 16:48

3 people like this

Dottie Harris wonders how many times The Monster has to fall backwards off the chair before he learns standing on it is not a good idea?

December 29, 2009 at 18:11

9 people like this

Dottie Harris says happy 2010 to everyone she loves. Hope it rocks for you. xx

December 31, 2009 at 23:12

7 people like this

2010

Dottie Harris is making seafood chilli.
January 2, 2010 at 17:33
3 people like this

Dottie Harris is sad that it's almost back to reality time again, especially as she's all bunged up.
January 3, 2010 at 16:45
5 people like this

Dottie Harris is fed up with this having a cold malarkey, plus the snow, plus teething toddler and is deciding which hot country to move to!
January 5, 2010 at 19:47
3 people like this

Dottie Harris thinks it's getting silly now! She's on the mend, but the boy is on a slippery high temperature slope. :(
January 6, 2010 at 17:37
1 person likes this

Dottie Harris just loves tea.

January 10, 2010 at 8:33

1 person likes this

Dottie Harris is cold. Stupid snow. Stupid ice. Stupid winter. Stupid UK. Stupid Stupid Stupid.

January 10, 2010 at 11:09

2 people like this

Dottie Harris is having a nice big glass of gin and trying to think of a dinner that doesn't include melted cheese or garlic bread!

January 11, 2010 at 19:53

2 people like this

Dottie Harris has just ice skated up the path to her meeting. She's wasted in project management!

January 12, 2010 at 10:35

7 people like this

Dottie Harris thinks things are looking good!

January 12, 2010 at 20:44

3 people like this

Dottie Harris is high on hot chocolate and fizzy Vimto!

January 13, 2010 at 11:00

2 people like this

Dottie Harris is warming herself up with alcohol and poppadoms!

January 13, 2010 at 20:36

3 people like this

Dottie Harris has just witnessed the mother of all tantrums, all because her son wanted to keep his nappy on in the bath.

January 14, 2010 at 19:07

5 people like this

Dottie Harris is confused as to why she is up and awake by her own choice and the small, smelly, loud Monster who usually makes the decision for her is still asleep??

January 16, 2010 at 8:10

3 people like this

Dottie Harris has finished work and is now finishing the wine. Oh good. It's Monday tomorrow.

January 17, 2010 at 22:58

2 people like this

Dottie Harris is seriously cheesed off with the A1, diversions that just stop, being late to pick her son up, leaving her wallet at work and having to grovel to Mr. Toll Bridge Man. Luckily he was sympathetic and accepted 5p and a Polo.

January 20, 2010 at 18:58

3 people like this

Dottie Harris will not eat the ice cream in the freezer. Will not eat the ice cream in the freezer. Will not eat the ice cream in the freezer. Will not eat the ice cream in the freezer. Will not eat the ice cream in the freezer. Will not eat the ice cream in the freezer.

January 22, 2010 at 21:35

1 person likes this

Dottie Harris didn't eat the ice cream!
January 23, 2010 at 10:14
1 person likes this

Dottie Harris totally admits she wants a 4x4.
January 23, 2010 at 10:41
5 people like this

Dottie Harris wonders how she can always cry at the last
episode of *Friends* even though she's seen it millions of
times?
January 25, 2010 at 20:59
3 people like this

Dottie Harris has gone over the 3-mile mark and will be
slim as Victoria Beckham in no time!
January 28, 2010 at 19:15
2 people like this

Dottie Harris is nearly home but needs to stop for vino!
January 29, 2010 at 19:13
4 people like this

Dottie Harris Home. Wine. Jimjams. Done.
January 29, 2010 at 20:19
5 people like this

Dottie Harris has nothing to wear even though she's just
been shopping.
January 30, 2010 at 15:15
3 people like this

Dottie Harris scrubs up OK actually!
January 30, 2010 at 19:25
4 people like this

Dottie Harris is laughing as she briefly considered not having wine tonight. HO HO HO.
February 2, 2010 at 19:58
3 people like this

Dottie Harris - Half a day left, fa la la la la!
February 2, 2010 at 21:12
1 person likes this

Dottie Harris is loving being part-time baybay!
February 3, 2010 at 16:09
4 people like this

Dottie Harris wonders why she isn't lying in on her day off when the boy is!
February 4, 2010 at 7:41
3 people like this

Dottie Harris thinks the weather is getting a bit boring now. Sun please! Thank you very much. She's wanting BBQs & Pimm's.
February 5, 2010 at 10:33
7 people like this

Dottie Harris has a boy with a very poorly tummy.
Is a little bit sick in her mouth
February 5, 2010 at 18:33
3 people like this

Dottie Harris just committed an act of child cruelty. She offered morning milk in a CUP! Clearly an offence worthy of being locked up!
February 6, 2010 at 8:30
8 people like this

Dottie Harris is trying to think of things you can do when it's cold, wet and grim that would entertain a small child. The suggestion of a bottle of wine by the open fire in a country pub went down like a lead balloon.
February 7, 2010 at 10:16
3 people like this

Dottie Harris is hating the woman on the ASOS site wearing skinny jeans. Stupid, skinny, six-packed cow.
February 7, 2010 at 19:37
2 people like this

Dottie Harris is cooking garlic bread.
February 7, 2010 at 19:40
2 people like this

Dottie Harris has been up all night looking after a poorly boy. Day 4 of poorly tummy and high temp and totally off his food.
February 8, 2010 at 7:20
3 people like this

Dottie Harris has gin, and suddenly feels like all is right in the world again.
February 9, 2010 at 19:04
5 people like this

Dottie Harris feels a bit bad about how scared of the carwash The Monster was, but not so bad she won't try it again.
February 13, 2010 at 13:32
9 people like this

Dottie Harris has just had beautiful flowers delivered! x
February 14, 2010 at 9:24
6 people like this

Dottie Harris is maybe more excited about needing a new ironing board than she should be.
February 16, 2010 at 13:53
1 person likes this

Dottie Harris was enjoying being a domestic goddess until she discovered her son had emptied the contents of her Dustbuster all over the dayroom.
February 18, 2010 at 8:53
4 people like this

Dottie Harris hasn't been asked for ID when buying wine. In fact, there wasn't even a fleeting glimpse of wondering on the cashier's face.
February 19, 2010 at 11:04
2 people like this

Dottie Harris wonders how her son is still on a high in his cot while she's ready to fall asleep on the sofa?
February 19, 2010 at 20:07
3 people like this

Dottie Harris is stuck in standstill traffic and not loving it.
February 22, 2010 at 17:41
1 person likes this

Dottie Harris is very proud of her son getting a sticker *and* a star for TIDYING UP at nursery school.
February 22, 2010 at 20:10
9 people like this

Dottie Harris has just watched her son be sick on her husband's back and is laughing a bit.
February 24, 2010 at 7:02
11 people like this

Dottie Harris is pleased to only be on half a day. Weekend begins in 5 minutes!
February 24, 2010 at 13:11
1 person likes this

Dottie Harris is thinking of selling her son.
February 25, 2010 at 8:42
3 people like this

Dottie Harris had a restless night.
February 27, 2010 at 7:24
2 people like this

Dottie Harris wonders how she had about a million pounds worth of ironing delivered back to her on Friday, yet here she is, standing at the ironing board with a full basket needing to be done? (Well, she's actually sitting on the sofa pretending the ironing board isn't there.)
February 28, 2010 at 14:12
1 person likes this

Dottie Harris thinks she should put down the laptop and step away from the PowerPoint presentation.
March 3, 2010 at 19:51
1 person likes this

Dottie Harris is considering giving her son a phone charger and box of matches, and telling him to play with them as she's sure once they become attainable they would be considered pointless to him.
March 4, 2010 at 18:07
3 people like this

Dottie Harris is pleased to announce she's given in! The magic number of tantrums is 28. Just don't tell The Monster!

March 7, 2010 at 9:28

10 people like this

Dottie Harris says thanks for her lovely birthday messages. xxx

March 11, 2010 at 15:50

18 people like this

Dottie Harris is loving being at home on Fridays so she can watch the first Formula 1 practice of the season.

March 12, 2010 at 8:35

2 people like this

Dottie Harris is thinking The Monster's dinner of fish shapes, smiley faces and peas looks rather yummy and kinda hopes he won't want it.

March 13, 2010 at 16:19

5 people like this

Dottie Harris thinks it's unfair that her son is mocking her by laughing, dancing and playing whilst *on* the naughty step. Sod.

March 13, 2010 at 18:38

3 people like this

Dottie Harris may be a snotty wreck on the sofa after watching *One Born Every Minute*.

March 17, 2010 at 22:13

2 people like this

Dottie Harris is pleased that The Monster is able to play in the garden with less than a million layers on!

March 18, 2010 at 16:38

15 people like this

Dottie Harris thinks it's amazing how new bedding ensures a better night's sleep!

March 19, 2010 at 7:31

3 people like this

Dottie Harris wonders if there are any "under two" football leagues? It's time for The Monster to start paying his way.

March 20, 2010 at 8:33

7 people like this

Dottie Harris is thinking a Wispa bar in the bath might be the new Flake. Mmm, chocolate!

March 21, 2010 at 18:28

2 people like this

Dottie Harris just realised she's put The Monster in bed and was looking forward to a child-free evening, yet she's spent an hour looking at photos of him.

March 21, 2010 at 20:48

9 people like this

Dottie Harris will *NOT* be making a Ninky Nonk out of yogurt pots. Thanks for the suggestion though, CBeebies.

March 24, 2010 at 18:23

7 people like this

Dottie Harris thinks it is totally unacceptable that it's Sunday night already.
March 28, 2010 at 17:01
2 people like this

Dottie Harris has just spent 40 mins putting The Monster back on naughty step. Fun times. OR NOT.
March 31, 2010 at 17:17
5 people like this

Dottie Harris thinks she might sleep for a week.
April 1, 2010 at 17:26
3 people like this

Dottie Harris would like to thank her radiator for doing the job her washer-dryer seems incapable of doing. You know, drying clothes.
April 1, 2010 at 17:43
2 people like this

Dottie Harris is trying to sneak some car shopping into her day without her husband noticing what she's doing!
April 3, 2010 at 8:33
1 person likes this

Dottie Harris is packing up the car to send The Monster away for the night. Ahhh dinner out and a lie in tomorrow. Perfick!
April 4, 2010 at 11:59
3 people like this

Dottie Harris needed that lie in. She feels grim, and she only had one glass of wine!
April 5, 2010 at 9:45
3 people like this

Dottie Harris is full of lard. Healthy again as of tomorrow. Maybe.

April 6, 2010 at 20:09

5 people like this

Dottie Harris is pleased to announce that she's not just fat any more. She's pregnant! Even better: there is only one baby in her tummy!

April 14, 2010 at 16:31

18 people like this

Dottie Harris is considering not picking up or tidying up after her husband and son for a week just to see how filthy her house really gets!

April 18, 2010 at 9:00

7 people like this

Dottie Harris is sure the glowing stage was meant to have started by now and the curling up into a ball and wanting to die one should have stopped?

April 18, 2010 at 16:20

16 people like this

Dottie Harris has been having lovely cuddles from her son. <3

April 20, 2010 at 17:37

5 people like this

Dottie Harris is wondering when the phrase "Sit there until you can behave" started to translate to "Scream at me and destroy my lounge."

April 21, 2010 at 17:49

7 people like this

Dottie Harris thinks "Row Row" at 8 a.m. is not an enjoyable way to wake up!!!!
April 23, 2010 at 8:31
1 person likes this

Dottie Harris is hiding with the laptop and the credit card.
April 24, 2010 at 9:40
2 people like this

Dottie Harris thinks that you know you have issues when your son points to your stomach and shouts "BALL."
April 24, 2010 at 16:59
5 people like this

Dottie Harris is chanting DOMINO'S DOMINO'S DOMINO'S until her husband just gives in and agrees.
April 27, 2010 at 18:20
2 people like this

Dottie Harris is trying to get the energy to move from the sofa and make the house look less like a bomb has hit it (if she can stop crying at *Project Runway*).
April 30, 2010 at 11:16
1 person likes this

Dottie Harris is thinking it's all gone rather quiet in the other room. Does she dare go and investigate?
April 30, 2010 at 14:27
3 people like this

Dottie Harris has just had her boobs "honked" by her son. Time for a quick chat with Daddy about what wisdom he feels the need to pass on!
April 30, 2010 at 17:11
8 people like this

Dottie Harris is counting down the minutes to The Monster's bedtime so she can have a bath and maybe wake up a bit!

May 2, 2010 at 17:31

1 person likes this

Dottie Harris would like to thank ASOS for their generous maternity sizes. Now she's fat on her holiday without the complex!

May 4, 2010 at 18:07

4 people like this

Dottie Harris is relieved that the lady at check-in didn't charge her excess baggage for her fat fingers!

May 5, 2010 at 4:33

7 people like this

Dottie Harris is back in dreary old Britain.

May 22, 2010 at 12:12

1 person likes this

Dottie Harris loves the smell of fresh washing but hates the idea she might have to iron it. Hmm, to call the ironing lady this week maybe?

May 23, 2010 at 8:56

1 person likes this

Dottie Harris loved the smell of washing before the washing line collapsed over freshly mown grass.

May 23, 2010 at 8:58

3 people like this

Dottie Harris is enjoying a very lemonady rosé spritzer. It's just the same as the real thing, honest!

May 23, 2010 at 16:10

1 person likes this

Dottie Harris is achy and grumpy.
May 23, 2010 at 19:22
1 person likes this

Dottie Harris is back at work, but has no laptop so is enjoying drinking apple juice and writing lists.
May 24, 2010 at 7:47
2 people like this

Dottie Harris can hardly watch TV when the annoying Jenni Powell is on.
May 25, 2010 at 20:14
4 people like this

Dottie Harris is really wishing the woman opposite her on the train wasn't eating Burger King and is also wondering if she could steal it.
May 26, 2010 at 15:37
3 people like this

Dottie Harris is exhausted after working three whole days in a row!
May 26, 2010 at 19:33
1 person likes this

Dottie Harris is super proud of The Monster for spending the entire night in a big boy bed!
May 29, 2010 at 7:13
11 people like this

Dottie Harris thinks it's time to get a loud child to jump on his father so that they can all finallllly have breakfast!
May 30, 2010 at 7:49
2 people like this

Dottie Harris has the house to herself and is enjoying the chance to clean, tidy, iron and arrange things on shelves.
May 31, 2010 at 10:17
1 person likes this

Dottie Harris is pleased that Simon Cowell just thanked her personally on the BAFTAs.
Cough
June 6, 2010 at 19:49
3 people like this

Dottie Harris feels a distinct lack of privacy when from the other side of a closed door she gets applauded for doing a "wiwi."
June 10, 2010 at 8:00
4 people like this

Dottie Harris has learnt the hard way not to fall asleep at The Monster's nap time letting him sleep for longer than allocated. He's still not asleep yet.
June 10, 2010 at 20:30
3 people like this

Dottie Harris is looking forward to a time when she can go to the toilet without having to wear a colander on her head.
June 13, 2010 at 10:15
9 people like this

Dottie Harris appears to have brought the devil child back from the store.
June 13, 2010 at 15:59
2 people like this

Dottie Harris is taking bets on whether it's a pink or a blue baby?!

June 15, 2010 at 7:35

3 people like this

Dottie Harris is finally going to have a partner in crime. 80% chance of it being a girl!

June 15, 2010 at 11:56

11 people like this

Dottie Harris is making a list of girls' names.

June 15, 2010 at 13:05

9 people like this

Dottie Harris supposes she better wake The Monster up from his nap. Hmph.

June 16, 2010 at 13:30

2 people like this

Dottie Harris is watching *She's All That* in bed with a peach squash. What has she become? :(

June 16, 2010 at 21:31

5 people like this

Dottie Harris is watching Elmo being fed Nutella on toast. Messy.

June 20, 2010 at 6:56

3 people like this

Dottie Harris can't believe her son is having a tantrum because he can't wear HER new shoes.

June 20, 2010 at 9:18

7 people like this

Dottie Harris hates the A1, hates lorry drivers with their shirts off who think they can beep at you and shout smutty things, hates Chrysler drivers and is generally in a vile hating everyone sort of mood.
June 22, 2010 at 17:59
3 people like this

Dottie Harris would like to thank Cbeebies for entertaining The Monster and thus allowing her to fake tan. Let's hope it doesn't streak!
June 25, 2010 at 7:51
6 people like this

Dottie Harris can't quite believe she just sung and did the actions to the "Grand Old Duke of York", "If You're Happy and You Know It" and "Head, Shoulders, Knees & Toes" whilst in the queue at the supermarket. What little credibility she had is now firmly out the window.
June 26, 2010 at 12:56
6 people like this

Dottie Harris thinks maybe she should start ironing rather than just buying The Monster new clothes.
June 27, 2010 at 13:36
1 person likes this

Dottie Harris thinks she's missing the point of party-sized chocolate bars. She's not just having one small treat, she's having one of each.
June 29, 2010 at 20:16
3 people like this

Dottie Harris thinks it must nearly be October now, she's fit to burst already.
July 4, 2010 at 12:47
2 people like this

Dottie Harris has rebelled. Ironing back in utility room, lemon drizzle cake in oven, child in bed, milkshake being sipped. Now is it wrong she's chosen to watch American trash rather than grown up programmes?
July 8, 2010 at 12:36
6 people like this

Dottie Harris is wondering how it's a punishment when, on asking naughty child if he wants to go to bed, he responds with "Yes."
July 9, 2010 at 16:13
3 people like this

Dottie Harris loves her husband but does not love the fact that apparently she looks like a Satsuma orange.
July 11, 2010 at 19:01
14 people like this

Dottie Harris has put her new orange top in the bin.
July 11, 2010 at 19:39
21 people like this

Dottie Harris has had a long day, and now for the first time since she moved The Monster into a bed is having to do the 5-minute rule while he sobs. Blergh.
July 12, 2010 at 22:39
1 person likes this

Dottie Harris must not eat two large bars of Daim Milka.
July 13, 2010 at 13:42
3 people like this

Dottie Harris is lying on the sofa moaning about the pains in her bump and back.
July 13, 2010 at 19:56
1 person likes this

Dottie Harris is banning any more toys or stuffed animals from entering her house. There is honestly not enough room for anything else.
Dies in heap of half-finished toddler's bedroom
July 17, 2010 at 17:31
3 people like this

Dottie Harris wants a baby.
July 20, 2010 at 14:04
9 people like this

Dottie Harris has a mini banana and pecan breakfast loaf while she waits for the train. She thinks she's feeling better!
July 21, 2010 at 7:13
3 people like this

Dottie Harris 100 days. Eep.
July 21, 2010 at 17:06
4 people like this

Dottie Harris is buying shares in Gaviscon.
July 21, 2010 at 21:25
9 people like this

Dottie Harris is teaching her son all about classic Britney.
July 23, 2010 at 16:18
2 people like this

Dottie Harris has put The Monster to bed in his big boy room and isn't sure how the night will go.
July 23, 2010 at 19:17
1 person likes this

Dottie Harris thinks the big boy room is a hit. HE IS STILL ASLEEP! So why has she been awake all night checking if he's breathing?
July 24, 2010 at 8:11
12 people like this

Dottie Harris has a Mars ice cream in the freezer but can't decide when to eat it.
July 25, 2010 at 16:47
3 people like this

Dottie Harris loves that when she checked on The Monster, he was asleep on his sofa instead of his bed.
July 27, 2010 at 20:17
6 people like this

Dottie Harris is wondering if 12 outfits for 4 days is excessive?
July 29, 2010 at 18:40
2 people like this

Dottie Harris is going to Budapest baybayyyy!
July 30, 2010 at 6:52
7 people like this

Dottie Harris is back in the UK, but it's not so bad because there is a small Monster waiting at home! x
August 2, 2010 at 13:33
2 people like this

Dottie Harris and The Monster are chilling whilst watching *Project Runway*.
August 4, 2010 at 15:07
3 people like this

Dottie Harris thinks her vile mood is starting to calm down. She could really do with a bottle of gin or 10 though!

August 4, 2010 at 19:38

1 person likes this

Dottie Harris has spent the day baking cupcakes and building JCB diggers. The cakes were somewhat more successful than the diggers.

August 6, 2010 at 18:21

4 people like this

Dottie Harris is wishing her very special boy a Happy 2nd Birthday! Now pass me some bright red cakes.

August 7, 2010 at 7:11

12 people like this

Dottie Harris is very pleased The Monster's first day in the big class at nursery school went well!

August 9, 2010 at 19:02

9 people like this

Dottie Harris just needs to confirm something before it's too late: When she goes to collect the new baby from the hospital that's when they take away the horrible first one, right?!

August 13, 2010 at 7:46

11 people like this

Dottie Harris is wondering how she is expected to shower/dress/etc. in 20 minutes when her husband has only just gotten out of the shower after 25 minutes!

August 15, 2010 at 8:17

1 person likes this

Dottie Harris is thinking stupid cold train platform. Stupid cold England. Must check what leave is left so maternity leave can start NOW.
August 16, 2010 at 7:20
1 person likes this

Dottie Harris hates not being able to bend in the middle.
August 16, 2010 at 19:49
5 people like this

Dottie Harris really needs to stop thinking about buying stuff for the baby and actually start buying it before it's too late!
August 17, 2010 at 19:28
9 people like this

Dottie Harris is trying to work it out. If you have two kids and you're in the car park, do you put the toddler in the car first before it runs away or put the baby in the car first so it doesn't get stolen? *Freaking out*
August 18, 2010 at 6:28
9 people like this

Dottie Harris thinks if her husband continues to come up with stupid baby names she will just name the baby Tinkerbell Trixy Rapunzel and be done with it.
August 18, 2010 at 18:44
3 people like this

Dottie Harris is looking forward to maternity leave and giving the house a GOOD CLEAN. Or at least a wipe down before lying on the sofa doing nothing!
August 21, 2010 at 7:37
2 people like this

Dottie Harris is counting down the hours, minutes, seconds.
August 23, 2010 at 9:12
5 people like this

Dottie Harris is sitting on the sofa in PJs, with a cup of tea, *GMTV* and 5 mins quiet before she decides what to do with her first work and Monster free morning! Damn not being allowed gin!
August 25, 2010 at 7:27
6 people like this

Dottie Harris thinks if any more of those bloody seeds fly into her house over her cleaned/hoovered floors she's going to go and vacuum the entire park.
August 25, 2010 at 20:47
3 people like this

Dottie Harris had a huge supermarket delivery today but the only thing the baby really fancies is pizza.
August 26, 2010 at 17:38
1 person likes this

Dottie Harris - It's the weekend jump up it's time to have some funnnn!!! (Who got the CBeebies reference there?)
August 27, 2010 at 7:06
9 people like this

Dottie Harris isn't having fish fingers and chips with lots of salt and a small glass of wine for dinner. Nope. She's obviously having lots of green veg and water. Honest.
September 1, 2010 at 18:50
5 people like this

Dottie Harris is happy to announce that the drugs the doctor gave her are amazing and she slept like a fat pregnant woman, not an elephant in pain!
September 3, 2010 at 7:43
4 people like this

Dottie Harris thinks her son should be very grateful that his daddy is home as the line he's been walking on all day is very fine.
September 3, 2010 at 17:32
6 people like this

Dottie Harris is perhaps more proud than she should be about The Monster saying "loser" with the L on his forehead, and the *Friends* fist together, flappy arms action.
September 4, 2010 at 13:02
12 people like this

Dottie Harris has sent the boys off to nursery school/work, showered, dried her hair and made beds. However, the thought of getting dressed and cleaning all three floors seems like too much hard work. Maybe testing out the freshly made bed is an option?
September 7, 2010 at 8:05
1 person likes this

Dottie Harris has spent half the day "nesting" yet feels that nothing other than more mess has been created!
September 7, 2010 at 12:34
3 people like this

Dottie Harris may or may not have been stuck in the Tupperware cupboard for 40 minutes this afternoon.
September 7, 2010 at 16:55
11 people like this

Dottie Harris is thinking: If you were a set of cot bed sheets, where would you be?
September 8, 2010 at 12:34
3 people like this

Dottie Harris is officially too fat for the slides at the soft play. She just got stuck.
September 8, 2010 at 14:42
15 people like this

Dottie Harris thinks her dates are wrong. Surely she can't continue to be such a fatty for much longer?
September 9, 2010 at 11:03
6 people like this

Dottie Harris is at toddler football with a hot chocolate thinking this is her Saturday mornings for the next 16 years (unless he makes the England team before then, is that possible? Not a clue how these things work!).
September 11, 2010 at 8:52
7 people like this

Dottie Harris is not loving The Monster and his new-found freedom now that he can open his bedroom door.
September 12, 2010 at 18:58
2 people like this

Dottie Harris is still not loving it.
September 12, 2010 at 20:03
9 people like this

Dottie Harris is thinking it may be a looooonnnnnggggg day.
September 13, 2010 at 7:30
3 people like this

Dottie Harris has lost the will to clean. :(
September 13, 2010 at 12:08
5 people like this

Dottie Harris is getting fed up with this constant need to wee malarkey.
September 13, 2010 at 18:05
3 people like this

Dottie Harris is totally loving Wonder Woman on Lorraine!
September 14, 2010 at 8:14
2 people like this

Dottie Harris doesn't think there is any point in her bringing the plate of cake upstairs to the lounge when the cake is gone by the top step.
September 14, 2010 at 10:38
5 people like this

Dottie Harris has reached a new all-time low. Husband had to help her remove skinny jeans as she was too fat to bend and get them over her ankles. WHEN WILL IT END?!
September 15, 2010 at 21:16
13 people like this

Dottie Harris thinks it's great that she was left to discover on her own accord that they'd run out of baby wipes.
September 16, 2010 at 8:54
3 people like this

Dottie Harris is thinking she might have to go and sniff the gin bottle.

September 16, 2010 at 21:20

2 people like this

Dottie Harris is having to hide her McFlurry down the side of her seat while she sneaks spoons as there is NO WAY she's sharing it.

September 17, 2010 at 12:15

2 people like this

Dottie Harris is worried she might fall through the ceiling if she gets any heavier.

September 21, 2010 at 12:44

3 people like this

Dottie Harris is considering just leaving The Monster in his PJs and Ugg boots all day as that's what he wants to wear, and she can't be bothered to argue.

September 24, 2010 at 9:13

3 people like this

Dottie Harris has finally found something practical about being this pregnant: She can barely reach the sink to wash up! Hurrah for fatness!

September 26, 2010 at 8:40

9 people like this

Dottie Harris wants Toad in the Hole and doesn't care how many pubs she has to go to until she finds it.

September 26, 2010 at 15:21

5 people like this

Dottie Harris had Toad in the Hole and has cheesecake for later.
September 26, 2010 at 17:23
7 people like this

Dottie Harris wishes her son would understand that anybody in their right mind would love to be tucked in to their cosy bed and allowed to snuggle down and sleep for an hour!
September 27, 2010 at 11:51
6 people like this

Dottie Harris is hoping she'll wake up tomorrow to an immaculate house, all the ironing done, a quiet sleeping newborn baby in the crib and a flat stomach.
September 27, 2010 at 18:14
9 people like this

Dottie Harris wonders if using the phrase "Granddad will cry" to discipline her son is the wrong thing to do.
September 29, 2010 at 17:09
13 people like this

Dottie Harris had to put her son's vest on him this morning at the same time as his shirt. Not an easy job but at least it stopped the battle before nursery school!
September 30, 2010 at 7:49
2 people like this

Dottie Harris is unsure why The Monster thinks walking backwards towards something he's been told not to touch makes it all OK?
October 1, 2010 at 11:24
4 people like this

Dottie Harris has 26 days left until her due date, and is encouraging her fat daughter not to be like her father and leave everything to the last minute. WE ARE READY FOR YOU NOW, TINKERBELL!
October 3, 2010 at 8:55
2 people like this

Dottie Harris has given up on "nesting."
October 3, 2010 at 15:21
3 people like this

Dottie Harris was stupid to think that locking The Monster's Legos in the bathroom would encourage him to nap. How she didn't think about the other 8 million toys is beyond her.
October 4, 2010 at 13:06
5 people like this

Dottie Harris is adding extra spice to tonight's curry.
October 4, 2010 at 19:00
2 people like this

Dottie Harris - Door shelf on fridge containing milk and juice breaks and falls to floor + fatty who can't bend with no kitchen roll = pissed off pregnant woman.
October 5, 2010 at 18:36
1 person likes this

Dottie Harris is hoping that the mixture of CBeebies and Disney will babysit The Monster today.
October 6, 2010 at 9:05
2 people like this

Dottie Harris hearts *The Apprentice* big time. So many idiots, so many stupid statements.
October 6, 2010 at 21:12
2 people like this

Dottie Harris has just tried to rearrange the bedroom furniture. However, didn't get very far due to weak girly muscles and too many clothes. You'd think her current ass size would help her out.
October 7, 2010 at 9:11
2 people like this

Dottie Harris is thinking of just smoking it out. (Who can name the reference?)
October 9, 2010 at 7:23
7 people like this

Dottie Harris is hoping the excitement of picking up her new car (well new to her) and tumble dryer might just be rock 'n' roll enough to tempt this fat baby out of her!
October 9, 2010 at 12:26
5 people like this

Dottie Harris hasn't had the baby yet folks, no matter how often you keep texting.
October 11, 2010 at 23:11
15 people like this

Dottie Harris is lying on the sofa letting her son stick stickers on the bump. Anything for a quiet life!
October 17, 2010 at 20:45
9 people like this

Dottie Harris is still pregnant.
October 18, 2010 at 18:11
4 people like this

Dottie Harris is slamming doors and stomping up the stairs. COME ON BABY.
October 23, 2010 at 12:26
7 people like this

Dottie Harris is a mummy of TWO! Baby Girl was born at 14:51 weighing in at a chunky 9 lbs. 4 oz. x
October 25, 2010 at 15:57
27 people like this

Dottie Harris had the gin, the bubbly, the runny egg, and also the eating-breakfast-with-one-arm. Doh!
October 28, 2010 at 8:22
12 people like this

Dottie Harris is thinking size 0 by Christmas is unlikely given the fact she can't stop being a big fat pig.
October 30, 2010 at 17:50
1 person likes this

Dottie Harris has two little people fast asleep on her. It's just a shame she can't reach the remote to change over from CBeebies. Miss Hoolie is not good for her rage.
October 31, 2010 at 12:51
3 people like this

Dottie Harris has completed bath and bedtime. Time to put her "comfies" on and open the bar. G&T or wine?
October 31, 2010 at 19:25
2 people like this

Dottie Harris isn't loving the "toddler getting naked every time she turns her back" stage.
November 1, 2010 at 10:01
5 people like this

Dottie Harris is snuggling in bed with a sleepy little lady and finding lots of excuses to stay there!
November 2, 2010 at 9:04
4 people like this

Dottie Harris isn't eating Halloween chocolates.
November 2, 2010 at 13:23
1 person likes this

Dottie Harris must not turn Christmas present shopping into clothes shopping for her and the kids.
November 4, 2010 at 14:44
5 people like this

Dottie Harris is nervous. The Monster sneaked her can of Diet Coke away and used it to fill his tea set up.
November 7, 2010 at 17:50
4 people like this

Dottie Harris thinks that perhaps Auntie Mabel should put more effort into her song lyrics.
November 8, 2010 at 9:40
3 people like this

Dottie Harris - Caffeine.
November 10, 2010 at 8:06
12 people like this

Dottie Harris is disappointed that The Monster doesn't appear to be getting what a good idea an afternoon nap would be, especially if he wants to be alive when Daddy gets home.
November 10, 2010 at 12:40
3 people like this

Dottie Harris has just watched The Monster put his dinner in the bin. So not allowing him to use a grown-up chair again.
November 10, 2010 at 16:40
7 people like this

Dottie Harris thinks tonight is going to have to include alcohol and naughty food of some variety. If they all make it through bath time alive, that is.
November 10, 2010 at 18:09
4 people like this

Dottie Harris loves that on nursery school days her day doesn't start with kid's TV.
November 11, 2010 at 8:28
4 people like this

Dottie Harris has cracked open the final box of "congratulations" chocolates.
November 11, 2010 at 14:35
6 people like this

Dottie Harris has a poorly toddler with a high temperature and a very chubby baby with a slightly gunky eye. Where can she trade them in for cute, healthy models?
November 12, 2010 at 15:56
2 people like this

Dottie Harris is amazed how the person who had a fairly solid night's sleep (only interrupted by being told to come to bed when asleep on the sofa) is having a "well needed" nap, yet the person surviving on 3.5 hours is still awake doing chores.
November 14, 2010 at 19:23
4 people like this

Dottie Harris is shocked that there isn't a specific hospital for sufferers of man flu as it's obviously life-threatening.
November 15, 2010 at 15:48
9 people like this

Dottie Harris hasn't had caffeine yet, and it shows.
November 17, 2010 at 8:39
5 people like this

Dottie Harris is not loving that The Monster can now tell on her. He's already announced to a friend on the phone "Mummy ate my dinner." No more secret meals for me then. Traitor.
November 17, 2010 at 12:30
6 people like this

Dottie Harris is wondering if she can latch The Chubster onto the husband's nipple so he can do the night feeds and she can sleep.
November 20, 2010 at 22:39
9 people like this

Dottie Harris thinks poo shooter nappies suck at the best of times but half way through a cold, dark feed is the worst. :(
November 22, 2010 at 5:38
3 people like this

Dottie Harris loves her new washing machine a bit too much. Wonder if the carpet would fit in?
November 22, 2010 at 9:15
4 people like this

Dottie Harris can't believe her daughter has turned against her and is delaying gin o'clock with her insistence that she's still hungry (she's not) and that she's not tired (she is).
November 22, 2010 at 19:58
5 people like this

Dottie Harris is reconsidering revisiting her hamster-type bottle to crib feeding idea. Dragon's Den here I come!
November 23, 2010 at 3:34
2 people like this

Dottie Harris could murder a gingerbread latte, stupid colic.
November 24, 2010 at 6:42
3 people like this

Dottie Harris is reminding herself that her children are lovely, and she can't leave them outside, free to a good home.
November 24, 2010 at 18:41
3 people like this

Dottie Harris - Gin o'clock.
November 24, 2010 at 19:08
1 person likes this

Dottie Harris - Chubs, just because your nappies are disposable doesn't mean your vests and sleep suits are too.
November 25, 2010 at 8:54
3 people like this

Dottie Harris is excited about seeing snow in 27 mins if the BBC weather site isn't fibbing.
November 25, 2010 at 14:33
2 people like this

Dottie Harris has sick in her bra.
November 26, 2010 at 4:32
2 people like this

Dottie Harris just ooh'd because the CBeebies song has changed to winter. Bad times, bad times.
November 28, 2010 at 10:02
8 people like this

Dottie Harris is wondering how many cups of tea it will take to feel human again.
November 29, 2010 at 8:09
1 person likes this

Dottie Harris has opened the bar and is having a well-deserved drink.
November 29, 2010 at 19:32
2 people like this

Dottie Harris only has three teabags left.
November 30, 2010 at 8:27
1 person likes this

Dottie Harris is toddler free! For now...
December 2, 2010 at 8:26
2 people like this

Dottie Harris loves her kids so much more when they are asleep in bed.
December 2, 2010 at 20:01
8 people like this

Dottie Harris hates it when The Monster wants to help colour in HER picture. :(
December 3, 2010 at 15:03
7 people like this

Dottie Harris is disappointed she didn't find the remote control at the bottom of the toy box after clearing it out. It was her last hope!
December 3, 2010 at 17:27
2 people like this

Dottie Harris is considering running away to a hotel and sleeping for a year.
December 5, 2010 at 8:50
5 people like this

Dottie Harris would like to thank Ocean Finance for their fish tank television channel screen saver. It appears to be the equivalent of white noise for The Chubster!
December 6, 2010 at 9:03
2 people like this

Dottie Harris is wondering if every time The Monster has an afternoon nap, he has to do it on the landing.
December 6, 2010 at 13:14
5 people like this

Dottie Harris is being played by a 6-week-old. Sobs uncontrollably in her chair, coos and smiles in Mummy's arms. Mummy's a sucker for the coos.
December 7, 2010 at 14:29
6 people like this

Dottie Harris doesn't seem to remember a time where she didn't have sick on her.
December 8, 2010 at 8:39
3 people like this

Dottie Harris just turned round from doing the washing up to find a small naked child dancing to *Boogie Beebies*. He even managed to undo the poppers on his vest!
December 8, 2010 at 8:58
4 people like this

Dottie Harris regrets telling The Chubster that she likes newly washed and ironed bedding, as she now obviously thinks it's her duty to ensure hers gets washed daily.
December 9, 2010 at 4:08
2 people like this

Dottie Harris - Pizza. Gin. Done.
December 9, 2010 at 19:53
3 people like this

Dottie Harris thinks she needs a new haircut. Maybe not something to be worrying about whilst being thrown up on.
December 11, 2010 at 6:03
1 person likes this

Dottie Harris is loving The Monster "driving to work" on the car-shaped bathmat.
December 13, 2010 at 9:22
3 people like this

Dottie Harris would quite like to smack perky Katy from *I Can Cook* around the face, maybe with a frying pan.
December 13, 2010 at 10:22
7 people like this

Dottie Harris has had the nightly task of deciding between gin or wine. This time she chose wine.

December 14, 2010 at 20:13

5 people like this

Dottie Harris - My daughter has just thrown up in my mouth.

December 15, 2010 at 18:24

9 people like this

Dottie Harris is not loving that The Monster can now climb out of his travel cot. She discovered this while at her Mummy's where she was intending to be looked after while she drank wine!

December 17, 2010 at 19:52

2 people like this

Dottie Harris thinks it's time to put the kids on eBay. The question is, bundle package or single items?

December 18, 2010 at 7:16

4 people like this

Dottie Harris is regretting buying The Monster some underpants and showing him. It's going to be messy as he refuses to wear his nappy now. :(

December 19, 2010 at 8:40

1 person likes this

Dottie Harris hasn't seriously thought about locking The Monster in the garage this morning. Nope. Not at all.

December 20, 2010 at 8:34

3 people like this

Dottie Harris is doing bath and bedtime solo, and counting down the minutes and seconds.
December 21, 2010 at 18:24
1 person likes this

Dottie Harris is trying to watch *Finding Nemo* but is getting a running commentary from a small boy.
December 22, 2010 at 13:56
7 people like this

Dottie Harris is wondering if Santa will miss the port that the kids have left out for him.
December 24, 2010 at 19:18
1 person likes this

Dottie Harris is secretly gutted The Monster hasn't woken up and found his stocking and Santa presents on the landing yet.
December 25, 2010 at 6:13
1 person likes this

Dottie Harris would like to suggest that all people who buy toys that need batteries that aren't AA should supply them to avoid disappointment. (From The Monster, not Mummy. The game looks like a nightmare).
December 25, 2010 at 17:10
2 people like this

Dottie Harris isn't ashamed to admit she is possibly enjoying The Monster's new farm as much as (if not more than) he is!
December 25, 2010 at 17:51
1 person likes this

Dottie Harris is a wee bit roly-poly after all the food she's eaten these last few days!
December 28, 2010 at 19:24
1 person likes this

Dottie Harris can't believe it's nearly 2011. Have a good one folks! x
December 31, 2010 at 21:55
19 people like this

2011

Dottie Harris thinks her daughter missed the "Lie in so Mummy can avoid a hangover" memo.
January 1, 2011 at 6:55
3 people like this

Dottie Harris has a love-hate relationship with bread. She loves to eat it but hates the fact it makes her fat.
January 2, 2011 at 20:22
2 people like this

Dottie Harris has just realised all her radios are tuned to Classic FM. Old. :(
January 3, 2011 at 18:55
3 people like this

Dottie Harris is trying to decide what to do with herself and The Chubster today. Clear out clothes? Food shopping? Finish off the Christmas chocs with all new *America's Next Top Model*?
January 4, 2011 at 8:47
1 person like this

Dottie Harris is having cold sweats. She appears to have run out of gin. :(
January 4, 2011 at 19:31
3 people like this

Dottie Harris - Note to self: Do not cross-thread bottle and nearly drown child.
January 9, 2011 at 4:46
4 people like this

Dottie Harris has been trying on bikinis and has just been asked by her son why she has "two bottoms." Eleven weeks to build back that shattered bit of confidence then.
January 9, 2011 at 19:14
9 people like this

Dottie Harris really wishes she hadn't found The Monster "tucking" the cat into the sofa with her new cushions. :(
January 10, 2011 at 8:30
7 people like this

Dottie Harris thinks a bit of sleep and Starbucks coffee in the machine makes her very productive. Kids' clothes sorted, dinner in slow cooker, two rounds of washing done and five tantrums avoided.
January 10, 2011 at 10:58
6 people like this

Dottie Harris was going to make a curry for dinner, but is now wondering if she can use The Chubster's vaccines as an excuse to order pizza.
January 11, 2011 at 17:11
2 people like this

Dottie Harris is secretly wondering if she can get The Chubster her vaccines every day as she slept from her 11:30 bottle to 7:15. Whoopee!
January 12, 2011 at 7:59
6 people like this

Dottie Harris must not think about what shoes she's going to buy when she sells her son.
January 12, 2011 at 18:29
1 person likes this

Dottie Harris doesn't want to jinx it but 11:30-7:45.
January 13, 2011 at 8:26
6 people like this

Dottie Harris is tidying up the lounge and so far has found a toy rake, a toy chair, half eaten chocolates and a couple of snotty tissues all stored away in various nooks and crannies. Favourite place so far is behind the sofa.
January 13, 2011 at 9:47
3 people like this

Dottie Harris wants to know who told The Monster there was A MONSTER outside the skylight on the landing.
January 13, 2011 at 18:03
9 people like this

Dottie Harris wonders who the lady from *Mighty Mites* slept with to sing the theme tune of her own show.
January 14, 2011 at 11:07
6 people like this

Dottie Harris is drinking gin (or as The Monster refers to it: "Mummy Juice") and considering an Eric the Elephant and then bed!
January 14, 2011 at 21:16
1 person likes this

Dottie Harris is in bed with her ENTIRE family and is being body-slammed by a toddler.
January 15, 2011 at 8:24
3 people like this

Dottie Harris wonders if it's too early to have a whiskey. To cure her cold, of course.
January 17, 2011 at 7:51
1 person likes this

Dottie Harris is finding watching The Monster stab his peas and eat them one by one to be one of the most painful experiences of her life.
January 17, 2011 at 12:45
12 people like this

Dottie Harris thinks bath time running over schedule only means one thing: The bar will be open late!
January 17, 2011 at 18:24
3 people like this

Dottie Harris has 14 days until she's back to the real world!
January 17, 2011 at 21:06
2 people like this

Dottie Harris NEEDS to buy new clothes.
January 18, 2011 at 11:03
3 people like this

Dottie Harris is enjoying a peaceful cup of tea with the small fat one while the small horrid one is shipped off to school and the tall farty one is on the way to work.
January 19, 2011 at 8:41
11 people like this

Dottie Harris is going to sit in the shed to drink her wine if The Monster doesn't stop screaming on the landing. It's not a restful drinking experience!
January 19, 2011 at 19:38
6 people like this

Dottie Harris is listening to her youngest snoring again. Not sure she can kick her until she rolls onto her side like she does her Daddy.
January 19, 2011 at 23:25
2 people like this

Dottie Harris - Caffeine.
January 20, 2011 at 8:12
5 people like this

Dottie Harris has just been told to sit down and eat her toast properly. By her 2-year-old son.
January 20, 2011 at 8:17
4 people like this

Dottie Harris thinks the naughty spot should include superglue to ensure the naughty child stays stuck to it.
January 20, 2011 at 11:09
8 people like this

Dottie Harris feels a bit guilty that she's just convinced The Monster that making Angel Delight is baking.
January 20, 2011 at 15:04
5 people like this

Dottie Harris has a feeling a horrible, snotty, tear-stained child is asleep on the top floor landing. HURRAH GIN TIME!
January 20, 2011 at 19:24
11 people like this

Dottie Harris isn't quite sure her husband understands the concept of giving her a lie in. Bringing the kids to bed, turning on the TV and moaning about how tired he is doesn't cut it.
January 22, 2011 at 8:44
5 people like this

Dottie Harris is not loving the milky sick pattern on her PJs. It doesn't look good, and it doesn't smell good.
January 23, 2011 at 8:03
7 people like this

Dottie Harris wants to know where the "dirty bogey" that was up The Monster's nose has ended up as it's not there any more.
January 23, 2011 at 8:45
2 people like this

Dottie Harris is wondering why she wanted kids again? Poos and screams during bath time. 24 mins left.
January 23, 2011 at 18:36
1 person likes this

Dottie Harris is hoping Diet Coke and tea will give her the strength she needs to last the day when she's already had "Uh oh Mummay, Mummay juice spill/I broke it/Mummay's purse all gone."
January 24, 2011 at 11:20
9 people like this

Dottie Harris is starving, but very proud that she scraped The Monster's leftover spaghetti bolognese into the bin (and covered it with coffee from the filter to avoid temptation!).
January 24, 2011 at 16:35
3 people like this

Dottie Harris is choosing carbs and gin over a run tonight. Fail.
January 24, 2011 at 18:48
5 people like this

Dottie Harris - Happy 3 months, Chubster. x
January 25, 2011 at 9:45
10 people like this

Dottie Harris thinks if she hears "No, Mummay!" one more time she may jump out the window.
January 26, 2011 at 11:23
7 people like this

Dottie Harris thinks it's a good job her kids are cute, because otherwise they'd be out with the wheelie bin by now.
January 26, 2011 at 20:32
3 people like this

Dottie Harris wonders if nursery school does 24/7 care?
January 27, 2011 at 7:13
4 people like this

Dottie Harris just finished dealing with mammoth toddler meltdown from inside NEXT to outside Asda Living, all because he wanted new shoes.
January 28, 2011 at 12:57
2 people like this

Dottie Harris has been super busy, but she's not quite sure with what!
January 28, 2011 at 19:02
3 people like this

Dottie Harris has a poo stain on her left boob. Well, not the actual boob, the lovely black top she's wearing. This does not bode well.
January 29, 2011 at 11:25
10 people like this

Dottie Harris is testing the work waters again tomorrow. ARGH!
January 31, 2011 at 19:54
10 people like this

Dottie Harris had a good first day back at work yesterday and is back with her monkeys for fun and mess today!
February 2, 2011 at 8:37
6 people like this

Dottie Harris - Favourite quote ever: "Mummy is hot hot gorgeous."
February 2, 2011 at 14:00
13 people like this

Dottie Harris hasn't seen the impact on her tummy after having salad for tea. She is still starving too. Fail.
February 5, 2011 at 20:30
3 people like this

Dottie Harris has just found the television remote after more than two months of searching.
February 9, 2011 at 11:44
5 people like this

Dottie Harris is wondering when 2 became the new teenager?!
February 9, 2011 at 18:05
4 people like this

Dottie Harris has plans to be a domestic goddess today. Unfortunately, they require shifting bottom from the sofa.
February 10, 2011 at 8:50
5 people like this

Dottie Harris - One word: Pancakes.
February 11, 2011 at 8:29
2 people like this

Dottie Harris has opened the bar with a glass of red.
February 11, 2011 at 20:06
4 people like this

Dottie Harris - This morning is sponsored by tea.
February 12, 2011 at 8:28
5 people like this

Dottie Harris is eating a Creme Egg and reading Elle while watching The Monster and Daddy play in soft play hell. Well, not watching them at all. She's looking after the baby!
February 13, 2011 at 12:51
3 people like this

Dottie Harris doesn't really enjoy the feeling of baby sick in the cup of her hand but at least the bedding is saved.
February 15, 2011 at 18:26
4 people like this

Dottie Harris is disappointed The Chubster doesn't like baby porridge.

February 18, 2011 at 8:13

1 person likes this

Dottie Harris is considering hiding from her children in the loft.

February 18, 2011 at 17:17

5 people like this

Dottie Harris is meant to be doing some work tonight. However, the wine is calling. Argh! Decisions, decisions!

February 20, 2011 at 20:02

1 person likes this

Dottie Harris is feeling a little bit soppy after The Monster told her he was "Berry Appy" today.

February 20, 2011 at 20:38

9 people like this

Dottie Harris has opened the bar a whole hour late.

February 22, 2011 at 20:02

5 people like this

Dottie Harris has no children for another hour (thank goodness for sleepovers at The Outlaws) and is intending to take a shower without somebody hammering on the door and screaming.

February 23, 2011 at 8:49

5 people like this

Dottie Harris thinks it's amazing how long you'll put up with being kicked in the head when it means you can stay in bed.

February 26, 2011 at 7:31

11 people like this

Dottie Harris - Dear Chubster. Please stop snoring, it's doing my head in.
February 28, 2011 at 23:52

5 people like this

Dottie Harris won't bother coming home from work again if she continues to be greeted by tantrums, sick and a late opening to the bar.
March 2, 2011 at 19:25

3 people like this

Dottie Harris just had her last Friday at home with the kids. Next week, FREEDOM!
March 4, 2011 at 18:13

3 people like this

Dottie Harris is unsure where her son has learnt to "smack his ass" when dancing. Slightly worrying.
March 5, 2011 at 17:06

9 people like this

Dottie Harris knows everything is going to be OK. She has gin.
March 7, 2011 at 19:53

7 people like this

Dottie Harris might as well just stay awake all night.
March 7, 2011 at 23:17

2 people like this

Dottie Harris has stuffed crust pizza.
March 9, 2011 at 19:52

3 people like this

Dottie Harris has her eye on a classy combination of Mini Eggs and a glass of Merlot.
March 10, 2011 at 19:02
6 people like this

Dottie Harris has just been told by a 2-year-old to sit down and eat her sandwich. Happy Birthday to me.
March 11, 2011 at 12:10
5 people like this

Dottie Harris thinks The Chubster could have made the effort to stay asleep through her dinner to make up for the "impromptu bath in Costa's sink due to poo" debacle earlier.
March 12, 2011 at 17:38
9 people like this

Dottie Harris is thinking thank God it's only 5 more minutes until she opens the bar! It's been a long, poo- and tantrum-filled day.
March 12, 2011 at 18:56
5 people like this

Dottie Harris isn't abusing the Calpol recommendations to try and enhance sleep. Honest!
March 12, 2011 at 23:34
5 people like this

Dottie Harris is putting the kids to bed early.
March 13, 2011 at 18:29
2 people like this

Dottie Harris has gin and isn't afraid to use (drink) it.
March 13, 2011 at 19:39
2 people like this

Dottie Harris was going to keep the bar shut tonight.
However, a glass of red may help her speed email!
March 14, 2011 at 19:52
1 person likes this

Dottie Harris has caught the family cold but refuses to
moan about it, just to prove a point.
March 15, 2011 at 20:08
6 people like this

Dottie Harris really wishes the scales wouldn't say
ERROR every time she stands on them.
March 19, 2011 at 10:48
3 people like this

Dottie Harris doesn't think she achieved much today.
March 21, 2011 at 19:44
1 person likes this

Dottie Harris hates that feeling when you find damp
pants on a toddler, but have no idea where the puddle to
go with it is.
March 22, 2011 at 18:05
9 people like this

Dottie Harris is putting out a warning: She's a wee bit
grumpy today. BUT NOBODY MENTION WEE.
March 23, 2011 at 8:43
4 people like this

Dottie Harris is pleased tonight's holiday packing is
sponsored by gin and chips.
March 23, 2011 at 20:13
4 people like this

Dottie Harris has just been to the bakery, and wonders if she could have her self-respect returned, please?
March 24, 2011 at 13:43
7 people like this

Dottie Harris wants to thank Ryanair for their superb suggestion that the 2-year-old sits about five seats away from each of his parents "so they can redistribute the weight of the plane." Practical.
April 2, 2011 at 15:34
5 people like this

Dottie Harris may be carrying a little holiday weight.
April 2, 2011 at 20:26
4 people like this

Dottie Harris is still recovering from the poo that landed on her foot earlier. Slippers are now in the bin, new ones on order.
April 3, 2011 at 17:03
9 people like this

Dottie Harris is having something healthy for dinner when she really wants Yorkshire pudding. Stupid bread and oil obsession on holiday.
April 3, 2011 at 18:07
1 person likes this

Dottie Harris is pleased that when she went to the supermarket she wrapped the bag of frozen peas around the bottle of rosé, giving it a head start on chilling.
April 4, 2011 at 21:21
7 people like this

Dottie Harris must remember that she loves her children—even if she has been awake for an hour and a half.
April 5, 2011 at 5:48
4 people like this

Dottie Harris thinks it's a poor show that for the second night in a row the bar is going to open late.
April 5, 2011 at 19:17
1 person likes this

Dottie Harris has opened the bar a whole hour and 10 mins late. Bad times.
April 5, 2011 at 20:10
2 people like this

Dottie Harris - Day 4 of the bar being opened late. Very bad times.
April 6, 2011 at 19:18
1 person likes this

Dottie Harris wonders what excuse she can come up with to justify that necklace she's just ordered online. She's sure it's the cat's birthday soon.
April 7, 2011 at 19:09
3 people like this

Dottie Harris is questioning her decision to have children.
April 9, 2011 at 5:49
7 people like this

Dottie Harris is the next celebrity chef, she just KNOWS it.
April 10, 2011 at 19:12
4 people like this

Dottie Harris Pox x 1 + Teething x 1 = Super Tired
Mummy.
April 12, 2011 at 5:41
2 people like this

Dottie Harris - To those of you who know me well,
what's your initial response when you hear I will be doing
racing experiences including a fast car, a rally and reverse
steer blind-fold driving? To those who don't, I can't even
reverse into a space. EXACTLY.
April 12, 2011 at 10:43
5 people like this

Dottie Harris confirms that no amount of makeup can
make a puffy, pus-filled eye look good!
April 13, 2011 at 7:25
1 person likes this

Dottie Harris thinks her legs might be falling off. (Not
exaggerating AT ALL.)
April 15, 2011 at 20:23
1 person likes this

Dottie Harris would like to know who dropped the
bomb on her house.
April 17, 2011 at 17:37
3 people like this

Dottie Harris is thinking it's only right to open the bar
with a glass of red since she bought new wine glasses on
the way home.
April 19, 2011 at 18:51
7 people like this

Dottie Harris wonders if The Chubster will ever be full?
April 20, 2011 at 18:03
2 people like this

Dottie Harris has gin, then Pimm's, then wine, then curry, then chocolate, then wine, then gin, then bed.
April 21, 2011 at 19:04
5 people like this

Dottie Harris is going to shoot the people who created the Lelli Kelly shoes advert.
April 22, 2011 at 6:10
7 people like this

Dottie Harris is wondering how many bottles of Nivea Firming Lotion it will take to firm her stomach up. She's also wondering if perhaps her "healthy" appetite is slowing down the process.
April 22, 2011 at 19:05
1 person likes this

Dottie Harris wants to go back to sleep. However, at 5:45 when she suggested to The Monster they cuddle in his bed his response was, "No Mummy, it's morning time. It's time to get up!" Oh.
April 24, 2011 at 6:25
3 people like this

Dottie Harris is wishing her little Chubster a happy half a year birthday, even if she's celebrating it with the pox. x
April 25, 2011 at 8:44
5 people like this

Dottie Harris has decided that chocolate for dinner is the way forward.
April 25, 2011 at 19:40
11 people like this

Dottie Harris - Today was sponsored by expensive foundation, Diet Coke and Tic Tacs.
April 27, 2011 at 19:09
6 people like this

Dottie Harris is super excited about "the" dress!
April 29, 2011 at 7:04
3 people like this

Dottie Harris has just told a sales call off for bothering her while she's watching The Royal Wedding.
April 29, 2011 at 10:53
5 people like this

Dottie Harris is fed up with using the phrase "Stop making your sister hit herself."
May 1, 2011 at 7:03
5 people like this

Dottie Harris is very happy to announce that the bar opened 4 minutes early. Good times.
May 7, 2011 at 18:59
3 people like this

Dottie Harris so hasn't just finished The Monster's Peppa Pig Easter egg in a pre-serious training and diet binge.
May 8, 2011 at 20:22
2 people like this

Dottie Harris wonders why The Monster turns all Oliver Twist when reading *Bear Hunt*: "It's a bbeewwtiful day, governor!"
May 9, 2011 at 18:53
1 person likes this

Dottie Harris may have got home from work half an hour ago but has already had 2 glasses of wine and a G&T. Average times.
May 12, 2011 at 20:25
6 people like this

Dottie Harris has just splurged in Paperchase and it felt GOOD.
May 13, 2011 at 14:07
5 people like this

Dottie Harris has just had the full impact of a Weetabix sneeze.
May 14, 2011 at 6:44
16 people like this

Dottie Harris is not appreciating the 'tude of a certain 2-year-old.
May 14, 2011 at 17:12
1 person likes this

Dottie Harris thinks "no wine on a school night" was a stupid idea.
May 16, 2011 at 19:35
4 people like this

Dottie Harris is very impressed—she STILL hasn't broken into her emergency KitKat Chunky!
May 18, 2011 at 19:03
8 people like this

Dottie Harris is thinking that when she said she wanted to paint the hall "biscuit" she didn't mean using actual biscuits. Thanks kids.
May 19, 2011 at 18:12
4 people like this

Dottie Harris doesn't want to have another discussion (tantrum) with The Monster about which T-shirt he is wearing today. THE GREEN ONE IS DIRTY, OK?
May 20, 2011 at 7:40
3 people like this

Dottie Harris - Note to self: Public toilets with a child? Don't go for the one facing the restaurant when the toddler can open the bloody door.
May 21, 2011 at 14:02
1 person likes this

Dottie Harris is already late for work and has a snotty, blotchy, tear-stained 2-year-old free to any home.
May 27, 2011 at 7:21
4 people like this

Dottie Harris is thinking The Monster is right on the verge of being moved into the shed. She's tempted to threaten that but knows she will suffer the repercussions of his spidahhh phobia. Next best thing? She moves into the shed.
May 29, 2011 at 16:28
7 people like this

Dottie Harris is wondering when boarding schools take children. Seven months?
May 30, 2011 at 7:08
4 people like this

Dottie Harris would like to thank the conjunctivitis fairy for visiting again. No, really. Thanks.
May 31, 2011 at 18:49
2 people like this

Dottie Harris isn't feeling the "power" today.
June 2, 2011 at 17:29
1 person likes this

Dottie Harris has discovered her life is getting fed back to nursery school via a small, opinionated, TRUTH-STRETCHING child.
June 2, 2011 at 20:14
9 people like this

Dottie Harris is perhaps too excited about using her new kitchen knives (on food, not her children).
June 4, 2011 at 15:15
11 people like this

Dottie Harris has opened the bar 10 minutes early. Perfect chance to review the new wine delivery!
June 4, 2011 at 18:50
4 people like this

Dottie Harris wishes The Monster wouldn't insist all of his toys "GO IN DA 'ALL COZ THEY BIN NORTY." She would also rather not hear him say to them, "STAY THERE FOR THREE MINITS TIL YOU CAN SAY SORRY" before slamming the door on them. Somehow, this may be an indication as to what the weekend has been like.
June 5, 2011 at 19:30
18 people like this

Dottie Harris and The Chubster are snuggled in bed with milk/tea watching *Peppa Pig*. <3
June 11, 2011 at 6:29
5 people like this

Dottie Harris is hoping to not be greeted at 6:30 a.m. with the cry of "Mmmuuuuummmmmmayyy, I need a poooooh!" Again.
June 14, 2011 at 21:18
5 people like this

Dottie Harris - Oh good. The Chubster has learnt that if she screeches 3 times in a row the light show projector goes on. That's going in the bin then.
June 18, 2011 at 6:42
7 people like this

Dottie Harris has opened the bar late. As The Monster would say, she's "not 'appy".
June 18, 2011 at 19:47
2 people like this

Dottie Harris thinks you know it's love when you're lying next to your daughter, and she throws up in your face.
June 21, 2011 at 2:43
11 people like this

Dottie Harris is worried that there are only 2 bottles of rosé in the garage.
June 23, 2011 at 20:04
1 person likes this

Dottie Harris is browsing a sports shop. And enjoying it.
June 25, 2011 at 9:14
5 people like this

Dottie Harris thinks The Chubster is a traitor saying DADA first. It's a stab in the heart.
June 28, 2011 at 19:03
6 people like this

Dottie Harris is going on a *Bear Hunt*. Again.
June 30, 2011 at 18:41
3 people like this

Dottie Harris is laughing that today, when The Monster "sprinkled" on his shorts while weeing on the grass, he insisted on hanging them on the line as they were "a bit wet now and need to dry off."
July 4, 2011 at 19:04
12 people like this

Dottie Harris thinks cake would be perfection.
July 5, 2011 at 12:41
5 people like this

Dottie Harris thinks it must be nearly wine o'clock by now?
July 8, 2011 at 7:34
4 people like this

Dottie Harris wonders why her children insist on team building and working together to prevent her from sleeping.
July 9, 2011 at 6:35
7 people like this

Dottie Harris has a feeling The Monster will be falling asleep on the landing again tonight.
July 10, 2011 at 18:28
3 people like this

Dottie Harris is thinking about calling the hall "The Monster's room" since he spends so much time in it. Note to self: Keep nappies and wipes in kitchen so as not to be trapped by naughty toddler with stinky baby.
July 11, 2011 at 7:43
5 people like this

Dottie Harris is regretting getting the paints out.
July 11, 2011 at 9:57
3 people like this

Dottie Harris would like to apologise to everyone in a 3-mile radius for the noise. She wasn't killing her son, just asking him to get dressed.
July 12, 2011 at 8:01
4 people like this

Dottie Harris is very happy now that her bumper pack of Diet Coke has arrived.
July 13, 2011 at 14:43
4 people like this

Dottie Harris thinks everything is forgiven when you hear "mumma" for the first time, even if it is at 4:23 a.m.
July 15, 2011 at 6:51
27 people like this

Dottie Harris has sent her husband out to buy an emergency bottle of gin and some limes.
July 15, 2011 at 18:32
2 people like this

Dottie Harris is bored of the word "mumma" now.
July 17, 2011 at 6:59
2 people like this

Dottie Harris is a calm, serene mummy. Nothing can faze, upset or bother her. Except her children.
July 17, 2011 at 16:55
9 people like this

Dottie Harris is officially self-employed. What has she done?!
July 22, 2011 at 19:22
7 people like this

Dottie Harris is suffering from DWT syndrome and needs a gin. (DWT=DAY WITH TODDLER)
July 24, 2011 at 18:52
1 person likes this

Dottie Harris is on mission: *Toy Story* Birthday Party. She's also a little bit scared about the cake she's decided to create.
July 25, 2011 at 19:19
3 people like this

Dottie Harris has found a new tooth in The Chubster's mouth. That explains a lot!
July 26, 2011 at 7:09
4 people like this

Dottie Harris has decided to swap the horrible nasty toddler for a nice quiet one when she picks The Chubster up from nursery school tonight.
July 27, 2011 at 7:09
3 people like this

Dottie Harris needs to remember that turmeric stains.
July 27, 2011 at 16:05
1 person likes this

Dottie Harris wishes her children would shush just a little bit pre-coffee.
July 30, 2011 at 7:31
5 people like this

Dottie Harris is battered, bruised, beaten and has a torn top after the mother of all toddler tantrums.
July 30, 2011 at 16:52
7 people like this

Dottie Harris has just been told by an almost 3-year-old he wants salad for lunch. He's still having chips.
August 1, 2011 at 10:31
8 people like this

Dottie Harris is excited. She is celebrating with a cup of tea SITTING DOWN because both children aren't here!
August 2, 2011 at 7:46
9 people like this

Dottie Harris is wondering if two Activias cancel out cake?
August 2, 2011 at 14:42
3 people like this

Dottie Harris has just caught The Chubster painting her teeth with lipstick.
August 3, 2011 at 7:03
5 people like this

Dottie Harris is needing all her creative vibes to ensure she decorates a birthday cake fit for a party that nursery school mums will be attending.
August 4, 2011 at 7:10
5 people like this

Dottie Harris thinks that all cakes and their decorating paraphernalia can just sod off. (Not that she's having a strop.)

August 4, 2011 at 12:59

2 people like this

Dottie Harris can't believe it but she's managed to not break The Monster for 3 WHOLE YEARS! x

August 7, 2011 at 6:32

23 people like this

Dottie Harris still can't believe she had a 20-minute conversation with The Monster about MOTHS at 3 a.m.

August 8, 2011 at 9:03

5 people like this

Dottie Harris is wondering what part of her thought it would be a good idea to not drink alcohol on week nights, you know, when she's had both the kids at home to herself.

August 8, 2011 at 18:10

1 person likes this

Dottie Harris is feeling rather sad for Elmo and Postman Pat (in a *Toy Story*-esque way) as they have been unceremoniously dumped for Buzz and Woody.

August 9, 2011 at 17:52

4 people like this

Dottie Harris - Dear Chubs, I'm sorry your teeth hurt, but Mummy is super sleepy so if you could suffer in silence I'd really appreciate it. Thanks. x

August 9, 2011 at 20:56

14 people like this

Dottie Harris is procrastinating.
August 10, 2011 at 15:52
2 people like this

Dottie Harris is sending her children to nursery school and going back to bed. Well, if they wake up ALL BLOODY NIGHT what do you expect?!
August 11, 2011 at 7:19
2 people like this

Dottie Harris is wondering exactly how many times it will take before her husband understands the following laundry concepts:
- light
- dark
- hand wash only
- do not tumble dry
- ironing vs. non-ironing pile
August 14, 2011 at 18:39
10 people like this

Dottie Harris has put her first headache to bed. One more to go, then time to crack open the gin.
August 15, 2011 at 17:49
2 people like this

Dottie Harris is trying to relax with a cup of tea but keeps finding toys behind the cushions.
August 18, 2011 at 8:09
2 people like this

Dottie Harris is thinking that since the box says "mini" and "Weight Watchers," the cake she's having with her cup of tea is the same as having an apple.
August 23, 2011 at 12:46
7 people like this

Dottie Harris is still laughing at The Chubster who ran over The Monster's toes in the baby walker and stole his biscuit!
August 24, 2011 at 17:49
15 people like this

Dottie Harris is using CBeebies and Nutella on toast to babysit again.
August 26, 2011 at 8:32
5 people like this

Dottie Harris thinks that the NEXT delivery guy is lucky he was bringing a present for her at 7 a.m. with his perky jolliness, otherwise she'd have scratched his eyes right out!
August 27, 2011 at 7:03
7 people like this

Dottie Harris loves her children today. (Sleep happened ALL night.)
September 3, 2011 at 7:53
14 people like this

Dottie Harris NEVER refers to The Monster as her baby but "WAHHH MY BABY IS GROWING UP AND IS AT PRE-SCHOOL TODAY!" This time next year, she may be a wreck.
September 5, 2011 at 7:28
5 people like this

Dottie Harris wants to know if it's the done thing to hit the "bigger boy" who hit your child at pre-school. By hit, she means trip over.
September 5, 2011 at 18:29
8 people like this

Dottie Harris has a feeling it's going to be one of those nights. Luckily, a week in the sun should fix it.

September 6, 2011 at 21:04

1 person likes this

Dottie Harris had a super (if slightly lacking in sleep) holiday with her little family. Now if she could just convince her husband to buy that villa round the corner from the beach.

September 12, 2011 at 15:05

7 people like this

Dottie Harris didn't just air-punch as her husband and the kids left the house. Honest.

September 15, 2011 at 7:05

14 people like this

Dottie Harris feels it's important to inform people that blueberry poo stains EVERYTHING.

September 19, 2011 at 8:11

5 people like this

Dottie Harris has just witnessed The Chubster being sent to the hall in her baby walker by a 3-year-old for 3 minutes for being "norty."

September 19, 2011 at 8:39

7 people like this

Dottie Harris loves it when The Chubster pulls a Houdini with the table cloth, a bowl of cereal and a cup of tea. The children were freshly clean and dressed for school. No, really. Good job Chubs.

September 20, 2011 at 7:45

4 people like this

Dottie Harris is amazed what a cheap date her diet is making her.
September 20, 2011 at 18:54
2 people like this

Dottie Harris - Surely 3 is too young to be selecting toys from the TV that they (you) are going to "buy today."
September 21, 2011 at 6:48
2 people like this

Dottie Harris has said "Well, if you lie down in front of the baby walker, you've got to expect to be run over by it" too many times already.
September 24, 2011 at 8:26
19 people like this

Dottie Harris just realised that this time next month she will have a 1-year-old. :(
September 25, 2011 at 18:16
1 person likes this

Dottie Harris thinks if The Monster says he's "too busy" at meal times one more time she SWEARS she will melt down on the floor.
September 26, 2011 at 7:48
7 people like this

Dottie Harris is witnessing The Monster eating his breakfast. So far it has taken more than an hour. The Chubster, on the other hand, has finished hers and has started grazing her way through the vegetable rack. *Sigh*
September 26, 2011 at 8:53
5 people like this

Dottie Harris can hear laughter and bangs from the lounge and is scared of what she will find in there.
September 28, 2011 at 6:22
3 people like this

Dottie Harris is mourning Ivan the iPhone. RIP Ivan. *Raises glass of gin*
September 28, 2011 at 19:31
5 people like this

Dottie Harris really shouldn't bake cakes when she's dieting and not allowed to eat them.
Wipes crumbs from chin and whistles
September 29, 2011 at 13:08
6 people like this

Dottie Harris is working out how childish it would be to not talk to The Chubster today (because she's been up every hour since midnight, not just for the sake of it).
October 1, 2011 at 7:51
9 people like this

Dottie Harris had a lovely day with The Chubster, The Monster and The Outlaws! Now for pink wine and sleepy time!
October 1, 2011 at 18:26
3 people like this

Dottie Harris is wondering how a child that refuses to crawl can cause quite so much carnage across an entire room in hardly any time at all!
October 5, 2011 at 6:37
7 people like this

Dottie Harris has just informed nursery school that she WON'T be collecting The Monster tonight, and they can keep the little toad.

October 5, 2011 at 8:05

3 people like this

Dottie Harris has just been told by a 3-year-old that he's not her best friend any more.

October 7, 2011 at 11:50

3 people like this

Dottie Harris is writing The Chubster's birthday list. She'd like a bottle of Hendrick's and some tan leather boots, wouldn't she?

October 8, 2011 at 15:05

12 people like this

Dottie Harris is hiding downstairs, leaving her lucky husband to deal with the disaster that is bath time.

October 9, 2011 at 17:17

4 people like this

Dottie Harris is thinking it's time to talk to her kids about their sleeping arrangements.

October 10, 2011 at 7:07

2 people like this

Dottie Harris thinks The Chubster could do with a mute button.

October 11, 2011 at 6:48

1 person likes this

Dottie Harris can hear the thud thud of a fat baby approaching. That's right, FINALLY she crawls!

October 13, 2011 at 7:07

4 people like this

Dottie Harris is thinking The Monster is pushing it. Delaying opening the bar for the 4th night in a row is NOT a good idea!!
October 13, 2011 at 19:22
2 people like this

Dottie Harris has FINALLY opened the bar.
October 13, 2011 at 19:40
3 people like this

Dottie Harris is being followed around by two loud children.
October 14, 2011 at 8:38
9 people like this

Dottie Harris is wondering if the stair gates will be able to hold The Chubster's weight much longer.
October 17, 2011 at 8:59
3 people like this

Dottie Harris thinks it's a little insulting that The Chubster keeps picking up the cow from her farm and saying "Mumma."
October 18, 2011 at 14:26
4 people like this

Dottie Harris has finally got her poorly baby back to sleep after nearly 2 hours. She, however, is now wide awake.
October 19, 2011 at 2:28
1 person likes this

Dottie Harris is wondering if there is such a thing as "Boarding Pre-School." Pass the gin.
October 19, 2011 at 18:01
8 people like this

Dottie Harris is more tired than she ever thought she could be. She thinks The Chubster might need to take her to buy some winter boots as an apology.
October 20, 2011 at 7:14
8 people like this

Dottie Harris is a domestic goddess: Crumble baking in one oven, beef roasting in the other, two different children's farms laid out. Just don't look at the piles of toys spread throughout the house.
October 21, 2011 at 14:12
10 people like this

Dottie Harris - Note to all parents who have those pens with magnets at the end: Check your radiators before you turn them on.
Cleans up massive ink slide
October 23, 2011 at 17:47
1 person likes this

Dottie Harris likes her children this morning so is rewarding them with breakfast.
October 24, 2011 at 7:25
12 people like this

Dottie Harris likes her husband today, therefore is rewarding him with dinner and a (small) glass of wine.
October 24, 2011 at 18:57
8 people like this

Dottie Harris no longer has a baby, but TWO toddlers. Happy Birthday Big Fat Chubster. x
October 25, 2011 at 07:34
19 people like this

Dottie Harris really wishes she'd not caught her daughter licking the toilet.

October 26, 2011 at 13:32

9 people like this

Dottie Harris supposes she better get ready to go collect her children. Apparently nursery school doesn't take kindly to them being left there overnight. Selfish much?

October 26, 2011 at 16:30

2 people like this

Dottie Harris wishes her children would stop body-slamming her.

October 29, 2011 at 6:54

1 person likes this

Dottie Harris made the foolish decision to show The Monster a *Spider-Man* cartoon today. She was hoping he'd hate it. He loves it.

October 29, 2011 at 17:25

3 people like this

Dottie Harris has decided that next year she will NOT be changing the clocks.

October 30, 2011 at 5:08

3 people like this

Dottie Harris thinks she will put a roof on The Chubster's cot if she attempts to escape from it at 4:40 a.m. again.

October 31, 2011 at 7:58

4 people like this

Dottie Harris is trying to explain to The Chubster that it is NOT time to get up for the day.

November 1, 2011 at 4:50

3 people like this

Dottie Harris is hiding behind the ironing pile hoping the kids can make their own way to nursery/pre-school.

November 1, 2011 at 8:44

1 person likes this

Dottie Harris has the horrors back from nursery school and loves that they are having tea quietly ON THEIR OWN. She just wishes she hadn't given The Chubster a ceramic plate.

November 1, 2011 at 16:42

3 people like this

Dottie Harris and the kids *may* have just polished off a whole packet of crumpets.

November 3, 2011 at 16:56

4 people like this

Dottie Harris loves gin.

November 4, 2011 at 19:46

11 people like this

Dottie Harris is feeling a mixture of guilt and pride. The Monster has watched approximately 6 (maybe 10) episodes of *Justin's House*. However, he's also just come through and said "Excuse me Mummy, sorry to bother you."

November 5, 2011 at 11:54

20 people like this

Dottie Harris loves her children. However, she wishes she wouldn't step in something sticky every time she walks near the table.

November 8, 2011 at 20:26

6 people like this

Dottie Harris is encouraging the world to embrace her new fashion trend: mismatched socks. Then her children won't look out of place.
November 10, 2011 at 14:52
6 people like this

Dottie Harris would like to replace her legs for ones that don't ache, and her belly for one that doesn't wobble.
November 15, 2011 at 16:54
5 people like this

Dottie Harris thinks it must surely be nearly Rioja-o-clocka?
November 16, 2011 at 16:32
5 people like this

Dottie Harris is trying to scrape Weetabix, dried banana and what she can only assume to be blueberries off the high chair in a vain attempt to make her house look less like a dirt bomb has hit it.
November 17, 2011 at 9:15
1 person likes this

Dottie Harris is regretting planning salad for dinner tonight. STUPID idea.
November 18, 2011 at 16:51
2 people like this

Dottie Harris is making a curry.
November 18, 2011 at 19:57
9 people like this

Dottie Harris is loving the karma of The Monster hating The Chubster watching him on the toilet.
November 19, 2011 at 9:23
10 people like this

Dottie Harris is wondering if her daughter is the only child in the world to be scared of the second verse of "Row Row"?
November 21, 2011 at 12:43
3 people like this

Dottie Harris thinks it should be against the law for anybody to speak, babble or cry until she's had her first cup of tea.
November 22, 2011 at 7:53
8 people like this

Dottie Harris thinks if she hears "Wait wait Mummy, I want... SOMEFIN" at bedtime one more time she'll have to turn to alcohol. Oh.
November 23, 2011 at 19:03
6 people like this

Dottie Harris has just witnessed a full scale fight between the children. She thinks The Chubster won.
November 24, 2011 at 17:26
4 people like this

Dottie Harris might hit her husband with her slipper if he doesn't stop looking for pizza discount vouchers and just ORDER BLOODY DINNER!
November 25, 2011 at 20:17
6 people like this

Dottie Harris thinks it's a good job The Chubster is cute or she'd be leaving her at the charity shop today.
November 26, 2011 at 8:40
7 people like this

Dottie Harris thinks her children must really hate her. Is it bedtime yet?

November 27, 2011 at 8:01

2 people like this

Dottie Harris is singing and dancing around the kitchen (much to the kids' bemusement). This can only mean one thing: SLEEP!!

November 28, 2011 at 8:39

6 people like this

Dottie Harris must learn to not eat brownies in front of the kids before they've finished their dinner. MELTDOWN! Rookie error.

November 28, 2011 at 17:01

7 people like this

Dottie Harris is beginning to think her obsession with taking photos of her food is a little unhealthy.

November 28, 2011 at 20:18

2 people like this

Dottie Harris has just gone back upstairs to see her son dressed in The Chubster's swimming costume and his Spider-Man mask. As you do.

November 30, 2011 at 19:58

21 people like this

Dottie Harris thinks the 1st of December means more than chocolate: Mince pies for breakfast.

December 1, 2011 at 8:30

11 people like this

Dottie Harris is quite impressed. She went Christmas shopping and didn't buy ANYTHING for herself.
December 1, 2011 at 19:20
7 people like this

Dottie Harris has 85 mins until the kids go to bed.
December 2, 2011 at 17:34
3 people like this

Dottie Harris - 47...
December 2, 2011 at 18:12
5 people like this

Dottie Harris is going to change her name so she's no longer the centre of "Mummeeemummeemummee" chants.
December 4, 2011 at 14:29
3 people like this

Dottie Harris - Phrase I never thought I'd use: "Stop hitting your big brother with that hammer."
December 5, 2011 at 10:18
1 person likes this

Dottie Harris had a very busy day and is looking forward to having a glass of wine to celebrate 8 years with her lovely (most of the time) husband. x
December 6, 2011 at 19:29
32 people like this

Dottie Harris is having another discussion with The Monster about how she doesn't think he'll be getting a Baby Annabel for Christmas.
December 9, 2011 at 8:27
10 people like this

Dottie Harris has yet again been stared out of the last waffle by The Chubster.
Sulks
December 10, 2011 at 9:18
8 people like this

Dottie Harris is a bit lost with The Monster still in bed. Time for another cup of tea and cuddles with The Chubster then!
December 19, 2011 at 9:11
5 people like this

Dottie Harris has used the "Santa won't come if xxxx" bribe 5 times in the last 3 hours.
December 19, 2011 at 12:50
11 people like this

Dottie Harris thinks her husband is treading on dangerous ground. His response to why he didn't pick up chocolate when requested: "Well, I thought you'd want to be good all week." Hmm.
December 19, 2011 at 20:41
3 people like this

Dottie Harris thinks there's a chocolate penguin in the treats drawer with her name on it!
December 19, 2011 at 21:16
5 people like this

Dottie Harris is still deciding if she made the right decision agreeing with The Monster that his snowman was alive. Nightmares a go-go tonight?
December 22, 2011 at 19:33
3 people like this

Dottie Harris is wrapping presents for Santa. Unfortunately, the elves are going to have to go out and buy some more chocolate pennies. Not Satsuma oranges, there are plenty of those.
December 23, 2011 at 19:44
9 people like this

Dottie Harris can't believe the most stressful thing about making a tiramisu is finding a dish to put it in.
December 24, 2011 at 11:21
2 people like this

Dottie Harris needs to put a ban on noisy toys.
December 26, 2011 at 6:01
15 people like this

Dottie Harris has just hit rock bottom. Her 3-year-old son let her win at "Snap." "Quick Mummy, shout it before I do! EHHHHYYY MUMMY WON!"
December 27, 2011 at 18:01
15 people like this

Dottie Harris was nearly just KILLED by a strategically placed Transformer.
December 27, 2011 at 19:23
15 people like this

Dottie Harris thinks the Tooth Fairy is a bitch.
December 29, 2011 at 8:22
4 people like this

Dottie Harris has decided *Ice Age 3* is this morning's designated babysitter.
December 30, 2011 at 10:28
8 people like this

Dottie Harris is counting down the minutes.
December 30, 2011 at 17:41
1 person likes this

Dottie Harris is more excited than The Monster about seeing the pantomime today! OH NO SHE ISN'T. (Oh yes she is.)
December 31, 2011 at 9:07
6 people like this

Dottie Harris is wishing all a Happy New Year. x
December 31, 2011 at 21:57
8 people like this

2012

Dottie Harris can't believe her daughter broke her New Year's Resolution of "LET MUMMY SLEEP ALL NIGHT" so quickly. Epic. Toddler. Fail.
January 1, 2012 at 6:41
4 people like this

Dottie Harris is playing pirates and treasure with The Monster. He's finding the treasure (Quality Streets) and bringing them to her to eat.
January 2, 2012 at 14:08
9 people like this

Dottie Harris is looking forward to date night. Only 7 1/2 hours until the kids are well and truly dumped.
January 3, 2012 at 11:30
5 people like this

Dottie Harris is so not eating mince pies and drinking tea instead of ironing.
January 3, 2012 at 13:34
3 people like this

Dottie Harris - 22 minutes...
January 3, 2012 at 18:38
6 people like this

Dottie Harris would like to thank the grumpy Sainsbury's delivery man for bringing her a bottle of gin. (As part of her order, not as a present.) It's going to be well used tonight judging by the current double child meltdown in the bath.
January 4, 2012 at 18:14
11 people like this

Dottie Harris is thinking "If you were a 3-year-old's PE outfit, and you weren't in your bag as expected, and you weren't in the laundry, WHERE WOULD YOU BE?!"
January 5, 2012 at 7:08
8 people like this

Dottie Harris is suffering from too much party food at this afternoon's toddler party.
January 7, 2012 at 17:56
1 person likes this

Dottie Harris is wondering why everyone is asleep except her. Perhaps the 3-year-old hogging her side of the bed is part of the problem.
January 8, 2012 at 7:19
6 people like this

Dottie Harris is hyperventilating. Kettle appears to be broken.
January 8, 2012 at 8:05
3 people like this

Dottie Harris is off to decide which school is unfortunate
cough lucky enough to get The Monster in September.
Sadly, none of them have boarding facilities yet.
January 9, 2012 at 10:30
9 people like this

Dottie Harris can't believe she's having a "mARsk" vs.
"mAsk" argument with a 3-year-old. Again. North/South
Divide already, REALLY?
January 9, 2012 at 17:08
6 people like this

Dottie Harris thinks today is going to be sponsored by
Benefit Playstick foundation and coffee. Poor Chubs and
her cough (and poor Mummy and her lack of sleep)!
January 10, 2012 at 6:57
3 people like this

Dottie Harris is thinking "Good night sun, hello moon!"
is the Best. Song. Ever.
January 10, 2012 at 18:01
15 people like this

Dottie Harris would have been out the door sooner, but
had to remove some of The Monster's train cars from
her shoes.
January 11, 2012 at 8:45
9 people like this

Dottie Harris has gin.
January 11, 2012 at 19:03
11 people like this

Dottie Harris is meant to be working but instead is crying at *One Born Every Minute*.
January 12, 2012 at 14:34
6 people like this

Dottie Harris is still in bed. Sadly, she's being body-slammed by two fat children.
January 14, 2012 at 9:08
3 people like this

Dottie Harris and the gang are off to buy a goldfish.
January 14, 2012 at 11:26
6 people like this

Dottie Harris never realised goldfish shopping would be so exhausting. Needing the exact shade of yellow was particularly trying.
January 14, 2012 at 15:43
9 people like this

Dottie Harris is relieved that Barry the fish is still alive.
January 15, 2012 at 9:12
13 people like this

Dottie Harris is pleased to be having gin instead of that soft drink malarkey tonight.
January 16, 2012 at 19:28
3 people like this

Dottie Harris thinks today is all about clearing out the room of doom. Baby section of eBay here she comes!
January 17, 2012 at 9:08
2 people like this

Dottie Harris has just been told she is to go to the hall for giving The Monster cheese on toast instead of cake. Can she bring gin?
January 17, 2012 at 16:39
13 people like this

Dottie Harris is looking forward to a time when nobody poos (then claps) at the dinner table.
January 17, 2012 at 17:01
9 people like this

Dottie Harris has just been punished for another rookie error: letting The Chubster climb into the craft box. That's right. Play dough and moon sand are currently a little soggy.
January 18, 2012 at 18:03
4 people like this

Dottie Harris thinks her son would like to thank the general public for saving his life. If they hadn't been there to witness the whole "leaving soft play debacle/meltdown/screaming fit" he may not still be with us.
January 19, 2012 at 18:38
2 people like this

Dottie Harris thinks tea for parents should be covered by the National Health Service.
January 21, 2012 at 7:01
11 people like this

Dottie Harris is deciding how to redecorate the bedroom. Don't tell her husband, though. He's blissfully unaware.
January 21, 2012 at 20:43
5 people like this

Dottie Harris wishes her poorly baby would get better fast. :(
January 24, 2012 at 23:19
2 people like this

Dottie Harris has just been told she's wrong and The Monster is ALWAYS right. This is not how it's meant to work in this house!
January 25, 2012 at 16:58
4 people like this

Dottie Harris and The Chubster are currently not on speaking terms due to the incredible dinner bowl throwing incident.
January 26, 2012 at 17:24
6 people like this

Dottie Harris hasn't just eaten the last of her daughter's Christmas chocolate. Nope. Not at all.
January 26, 2012 at 20:08
5 people like this

Dottie Harris Monster: Mummy I don't want to be Fireman Sam any more..
Me: OK, you don't have to be.
Monster: YEAH I do! Lottie said.
Me: You don't have to do everything Lottie says!
Monster: YEAH I DO! She told me!
January 27, 2012 at 8:23
2 people like this

Dottie Harris loves hearing The Chubster chattering away through the baby monitor. x
January 28, 2012 at 19:33
7 people like this

Dottie Harris is still sulking. Since her birthday is on the same day as Mother's Day, it appears her presents are all merging together. Not sure this is acceptable husband behaviour?!

January 29, 2012 at 10:08

5 people like this

Dottie Harris is making prawn vindaloo and pretending naan bread is low fat.

January 30, 2012 at 20:02

3 people like this

Dottie Harris is too sleepy for a running commentary. "Mummy, is this your bed? Mummy, your eyes are closed. Mummy, you're missing Thomas. Mummy, do you like it when I do that? Mummy, I can hear singing. Mummy, you have a smelly mouth. Mummy, I need a wee. What's that noise, Mummy? Mummy, it's dark in the hall. Mummy, I've turned your light on. Mummy, I flushed but I didn't need to wash my hands."
Weeps

January 31, 2012 at 6:39

6 people like this

Dottie Harris is very proud of her little Chubster. She FINALLY took some steps at nursery school today! HURRAH!

February 1, 2012 at 17:37

19 people like this

Dottie Harris is thinking of quiet things she can do to entertain the children until bath time. It's a bit chilly to lock them in the garage.

February 2, 2012 at 16:28

4 people like this

Dottie Harris wonders if ANYTHING will remove the rash cream bottom prints from her landing carpet?
February 3, 2012 at 18:35
13 people like this

Dottie Harris is watching *Spider-Man*. AGAIN.
February 4, 2012 at 11:21
4 people like this

Dottie Harris has seen the snow and thinks it can go away now please!
February 5, 2012 at 7:27
1 person likes this

Dottie Harris is super ready for bed.
February 6, 2012 at 18:28
3 people like this

Dottie Harris has just watched Weetabix fly across the room and land on the fish bowl. It's going to be one of those mornings.
February 7, 2012 at 8:17
6 people like this

Dottie Harris has just rewound *Waybuloo* to the part where the Pipplings get right "in your face" three times. It's official. It totally makes The Chubster cry. Better try one more time just to be sure.
February 9, 2012 at 18:05
6 people like this

Dottie Harris - 46 mins until jimjams, gin, Sherlock, nails, nachos and mini Rolos in that EXACT order.
February 11, 2012 at 18:14
3 people like this

Dottie Harris thinks mini Rolos are a huge disappointment.
February 11, 2012 at 20:02
8 people like this

Dottie Harris has just removed two HappyLand characters, a kazoo, a wet baby wipe and two dummies from her Ugg boot.
February 12, 2012 at 8:37
9 people like this

Dottie Harris would like to point out that when sharing a lift with Noel Gallagher, discussing the weather and using words such as "chilly" and "plummeting" does NOTHING for your street cred.
February 12, 2012 at 23:47
15 people like this

Dottie Harris is having white wine as she's so pathetic and weak she can't open the bottle of red.
February 13, 2012 at 19:08
3 people like this

Dottie Harris is a bit grumpy with her husband for actually sticking with the whole "no Valentine's gifts" malarkey. DARN IT.
February 14, 2012 at 8:10
7 people like this

Dottie Harris is totally not loving the "I'm well at home but not anywhere else" stage The Chubster is going through.
February 14, 2012 at 15:28
3 people like this

Dottie Harris thinks she really needs to stop doing her work in the kitchen. It's not good for her frying pan.
February 15, 2012 at 14:21
3 people like this

Dottie Harris has just picked up the kids from nursery school and was greeted with the phrase "Oh no, are you drunk again, Mummy?"
February 15, 2012 at 18:34
11 people like this

Dottie Harris is thinking the "think before you speak" theory needs to kick in. "OK Mummy, you carry the fat one and Daddy can carry the horror. That's me." Oh.
February 18, 2012 at 7:39
4 people like this

Dottie Harris has just completed a 4.57 mile run on Runkeeper. Gin.
February 20, 2012 at 19:47
9 people like this

Dottie Harris thinks toddler diarrhoea in the bath on a solo bath and bedtime is one of her worst nightmares.
February 23, 2012 at 18:08
11 people like this

Dottie Harris - My children hate me.
February 24, 2012 at 6:02
2 people like this

Dottie Harris is wondering what to do with the monkeys on a wet day? The Monster has requested a bouncy cARstle.
February 26, 2012 at 9:31
9 people like this

Dottie Harris wonders if CBeebies really understands the impact of removing *Show Me Show Me* from the 9 a.m. slot?! When is she meant to wee and eat chocolate without the horrible children bothering her?

February 27, 2012 at 9:03

11 people like this

Dottie Harris is wondering which of The Monster's girlfriends will propose today and take him off her hands?

February 29, 2012 at 7:58

3 people like this

Dottie Harris thinks that at 6 a.m. she really doesn't give a <insert swear word> how high Spider-Man can climb.

March 1, 2012 at 6:15

4 people like this

Dottie Harris didn't just fall over a cone in the middle of the road.

March 2, 2012 at 10:08

2 people like this

Dottie Harris is totally loving The Chubster's current repertoire of words: "ta" "daddy" "diddy" (that's me) "cuddle" "don't touch" and as of tonight "hedgehog." There is also the obvious shock that "pie" "cake" and "fat" aren't being uttered yet.

March 4, 2012 at 11:33

3 people like this

Dottie Harris has just witnessed her daughter lick the side of a cupcake, decide she likes it and shove THE ENTIRE cake in her mouth. Like mother like daughter.

March 7, 2012 at 13:36

9 people like this

Dottie Harris may have decided to roast some chicken instead of going for a run. After all, you can't run on your birthday, can you?

March 11, 2012 at 16:27

1 person likes this

Dottie Harris has been filming The Chubster's tantrum. She is currently on 11 minutes and counting.

March 13, 2012 at 17:25

6 people like this

Dottie Harris is pleased to note it only took 40 minutes for The Chubster to stop tantruming. What made her stop? The *Waybuloo* theme tune, of course.

March 13, 2012 at 18:01

8 people like this

Dottie Harris is very much looking forward to her 3 nights in the sun without her lovely but loud children!

March 15, 2012 at 19:23

7 people like this

Dottie Harris is a very lucky, very spoilt girl on the "Weekend of Dottie."

March 17, 2012 at 18:56

3 people like this

Dottie Harris has just witnessed The Chubster lick all the porridge off every teeny tiny bit of strawberry in her breakfast before discarding them all on the floor.

March 23, 2012 at 8:11

4 people like this

Dottie Harris completed a whole 10k run!

March 25, 2012 at 11:24

23 people like this

Dottie Harris is very sleepy.
March 25, 2012 at 18:31
6 people like this

Dottie Harris would very much like her legs to reattach themselves to her body please.
March 26, 2012 at 9:32
5 people like this

Dottie Harris really wishes The Chubster and The Monster would stop shouting at her from their bedrooms. Don't they know it's time to open the bar?
March 27, 2012 at 19:15
3 people like this

Dottie Harris - It would be wrong to respond to a 3-year-old who asks "Mummy, what's your problem?" with "YOU!" wouldn't it?
March 28, 2012 at 18:34
6 people like this

Dottie Harris is watching her daughter lie on the floor and head-butt the sofa, all because she wasn't allowed to open the oven. Looks like they are going to rock up to nursery school early today.
March 29, 2012 at 7:45
2 people like this

Dottie Harris wishes The Chubster hadn't been quite so forceful when saying to the hairdresser "Don't touch!" during her first ever hair cut.
March 30, 2012 at 11:23
5 people like this

Dottie Harris is off to the emergency room with The Chubster and a gash due to a "falling onto corner of the coffee table" incident.
March 31, 2012 at 15:08
3 people like this

Dottie Harris and The Chubster made it home. She is now tucked up in bed with a glued-together eyebrow after being very (not at all) brave!
March 31, 2012 at 19:32
16 people like this

Dottie Harris wishes chocolate digestives would stop jumping out of the drawer and making her eat them.
April 4, 2012 at 13:45
2 people like this

Dottie Harris loves her son's honesty. "You've got a big, fat, wobbly belly, Mummy." Thanks. No, really.
April 6, 2012 at 8:23
5 people like this

Dottie Harris would really like The Monster's temperature to drop below 38 C, even just for half an hour. :(
April 8, 2012 at 21:11
2 people like this

Dottie Harris had an eventful hour doing crafts, finishing with The Monster telling her she needs a shower.
April 10, 2012 at 10:18
9 people like this

Dottie Harris didn't really enjoy cutting her daughter out of a poo-filled sleep suit before her first cup of tea.
April 11, 2012 at 7:21
11 people like this

Dottie Harris is wondering if somebody will collect her children from nursery school so she doesn't have to go outside in the rain. :(
April 11, 2012 at 17:55
3 people like this

Dottie Harris is fed up with the daily "shorts and high up sleeves" vs. "jeans and low down sleeves" debate with The Monster already. COME ON SUMMER!
April 18, 2012 at 8:01
4 people like this

Dottie Harris thought *My Week with Marilyn* was amazebogs.
April 21, 2012 at 21:34
7 people like this

Dottie Harris has just discovered where she will be off-loading The Monster when he goes to school!
April 23, 2012 at 9:35
16 people like this

Dottie Harris thought the first time The Chubster got out of bed and stomped through to see her was cute. Five times later she's not so sure!
April 26, 2012 at 0:03
6 people like this

Dottie Harris has Chinese takeout and wine. All is good with the world!
April 27, 2012 at 20:01
5 people like this

Dottie Harris - One good thing about wet weather: Sunday Roast!
April 29, 2012 at 12:23
6 people like this

Dottie Harris - "Mummy, do you have a boyfriend?"
"Well... Yes... Daddy is kind of my boyfriend. Do you have a boyfriend?"
"Yes, it's called Lucy and Dylan. That's who my boyfriend is."
April 29, 2012 at 18:56
2 people like this

Dottie Harris is fed up with looking outside into the cold, wet, dark sky IN MAY.
May 1, 2012 at 11:29
2 people like this

Dottie Harris hasn't had enough tea to cope with the number of times she's been asked "Do ya know???" this morning.
May 3, 2012 at 7:47
9 people like this

Dottie Harris HATES Transformers.
May 4, 2012 at 10:18
4 people like this

Dottie Harris thinks if she hears the phrase "Let's burn some rubber on HotRod highway" one more time a toy car and two children may end up in the bin.
May 5, 2012 at 7:03
9 people like this

Dottie Harris had a lovely date night, and now that she's had a 10-hour sleep and McMuffin (with hash browns) is looking forward to getting her monkeys back. x
May 6, 2012 at 10:38
5 people like this

Dottie Harris thinks her morning cup of tea in bed would be much more relaxing if one child wasn't head-butting her stomach while the other is tickling her feet.
May 7, 2012 at 9:03
4 people like this

Dottie Harris is beginning to doubt The Chubster is her daughter. She just turned down a Milky Way for a banana.
May 8, 2012 at 14:13
6 people like this

Dottie Harris is feeling a bit sick after The Monster said he wasn't thirsty because he's licked the rain off his best friend's car.
May 9, 2012 at 16:02
5 people like this

Dottie Harris - Dear Chubster, if you don't sleep tonight I'm swapping you for pizza. Love you. Mummy. x
May 14, 2012 at 19:09
21 people like this

Dottie Harris thinks "has been a tad trying" is the only phrase she can use to describe the last two hours without somebody sending the social services around.
May 14, 2012 at 19:34
8 people like this

Dottie Harris wishes The Chubster wouldn't tell her she wants the television on in the lounge by hitting her on the head with the remote control.
May 19, 2012 at 8:11
4 people like this

Dottie Harris doesn't like to brag but thinks her G&T prawns are amazing!
May 19, 2012 at 20:48
3 people like this

Dottie Harris is thinking The Monster's potential school uniform is rather dull. Why not put a massive dinosaur on the front instead of a tree?
May 21, 2012 at 14:28
8 people like this

Dottie Harris is tired. Maybe the kids need an early night? FAT CHANCE.
May 21, 2012 at 18:01
2 people like this

Dottie Harris has two exhausted, fast asleep children, worn out from Nan and Granddad garden fun. x
May 27, 2012 at 19:23
3 people like this

Dottie Harris needs to know when the "getting every single toy out in every single room across the entire house all at once" (a.k.a. house carnage) stage ends, please.
May 28, 2012 at 13:58
17 people like this

Dottie Harris is regretting thinking "Oh a salad would be lovely tonight" and is wishing she'd bought pizza and chocolate.
May 31, 2012 at 19:11
5 people like this

Dottie Harris is starting to tire of telling her son to "put the mouse back in the house."
June 1, 2012 at 10:37
9 people like this

Dottie Harris is thinking that judging by the tantrum her daughter just had, she doesn't like dressing up as Fa... BATman.
June 1, 2012 at 17:08
5 people like this

Dottie Harris and the children are wearing paper crowns to celebrate the Queen at breakfast time. Rocking.
June 3, 2012 at 8:29
3 people like this

Dottie Harris knows the game of "chase across the landing" will end in tears but is going to sit back and see who cries first.
June 7, 2012 at 18:47
7 people like this

Dottie Harris really wishes The Chubster hadn't changed the channel to ITV2 then run off and hidden the remote.
June 8, 2012 at 09:28
4 people like this

Dottie Harris has actually managed to PACK LIGHT and is ready for SPAIN!!
June 9, 2012 at 23:16
9 people like this

Dottie Harris is enjoying the sun quite a lot, and is perhaps hoping it's raining lots in the UK because she's that smug.
June 17, 2012 at 11:08
4 people like this

Dottie Harris is still frantically working out how she can stay in Spain drinking bubbles by the BBQ.
June 19, 2012 at 21:19
2 people like this

Dottie Harris is not particularly happy about being home.
June 21, 2012 at 18:01
2 people like this

Dottie Harris discovered just how sore a loser she is after losing Pirate Pursuit legitimately.
June 22, 2012 at 16:29
5 people like this

Dottie Harris thinks if one more person asks if she is "sure" The Chubster is really not two yet, or randomly comes up just to say "She's a huge lass isn't she?" she may get stabby.
June 23, 2012 at 15:13
5 people like this

Dottie Harris is not happy about the new obsession with *The Power Rangers*. According to The Monster, her Samurai skills are in need of some work. :(
June 25, 2012 at 11:08
8 people like this

Dottie Harris is taking The Monster for his first school settling in tomorrow and is wondering if he can make it through the whole session without shooting web at the teachers.
June 26, 2012 at 19:57
23 people like this

Dottie Harris is enjoying this beautiful summer's da… Oh.
June 28, 2012 at 11:39
6 people like this

Dottie Harris has finally determined that when The Monster said he was "resigning" from pre-school he actually meant graduating.
July 2, 2012 at 10:19
9 people like this

Dottie Harris would like to point out to The Monster that even if you don't like the school uniform you still have to wear it, and no, Spider-Man suits aren't a better substitute.
July 5, 2012 at 17:56
5 people like this

Dottie Harris is very much looking forward to putting an overtired Green Gogglin to bed.
July 5, 2012 at 18:49
6 people like this

Dottie Harris has the kids in bed, 7 p.m. on the dot. Now for wine, STAT!
July 5, 2012 at 19:01
5 people like this

Dottie Harris has just been informed that The Monster wants a Ben10 party NOT Spider-Man. The only thing that can describe her current emotion: GAHHHHHHHHHHHHHHHHHHHHHHHHHHHH!
July 10, 2012 at 11:23
4 people like this

Dottie Harris would like to thank tea for helping her get through a particularly stressful episode of *Postman Pat*. Not sure who will win the race but excited about the final moral to the story!
July 15, 2012 at 7:35
11 people like this

Dottie Harris has just been informed by The Monster that he is "Fed up with putting up with my sister."
July 15, 2012 at 18:45
14 people like this

Dottie Harris went to the farm without the pushchair today. She now needs a takeaway and a gin to recover from THAT 40-pound work out.
July 17, 2012 at 19:19
18 people like this

Dottie Harris has just had to break up a bite fight followed by breaking out the antiseptic. Bad times.
July 21, 2012 at 9:23
5 people like this

Dottie Harris would like to apologise to the couple in the pub for the Ben10 water camera incident.
July 22, 2012 at 17:55
6 people like this

Dottie Harris really doesn't want to hear "Hello, Puppy calling..." ever again.
July 23, 2012 at 7:54
9 people like this

Dottie Harris is enjoying having her coffee without constant narrative.
July 25, 2012 at 14:08
3 people like this

Dottie Harris is regretting downloading "Let's Get Ready to Rumble" for the kids. Five replays in a row and it's starting to grate.
July 26, 2012 at 18:38
3 people like this

Dottie Harris really wishes her daughter would stop beating her son up.
July 29, 2012 at 17:21
2 people like this

Dottie Harris has just realised she's been wearing Ben10 socks IN PUBLIC. All day.
July 29, 2012 at 20:47
5 people like this

Dottie Harris thinks it's too early in the day to be hunting for lost pirate patches.
July 30, 2012 at 6:19
4 people like this

Dottie Harris isn't that fond of the name "Mummy" right now.
August 1, 2012 at 20:01
3 people like this

Dottie Harris has been jumped on by the heaviest toddler in the world. Winded doesn't cover it!
August 2, 2012 at 8:01
6 people like this

Dottie Harris has just been hit on the face by a slice of toast. Nutella side up.
August 3, 2012 at 8:32
8 people like this

Dottie Harris really does not appreciate there being toddler poo on her sofa.
August 4, 2012 at 15:26
7 people like this

Dottie Harris is doing frantic Amazon party decor buying.
August 6, 2012 at 10:01
2 people like this

Dottie Harris has a super excited 4-year-old! Happy birthday, little man. Glad we've managed to keep you alive another year. x
August 7, 2012 at 6:04
29 people like this

Dottie Harris is armed with gin and setting to creating a Spider-Man themed party.
August 8, 2012 at 19:36
6 people like this

Dottie Harris totally isn't broody after cuddling a GORGEOUS laughing baby. She also can't repeat what her husband said when she used the phrase "What harm would one more do?"
August 9, 2012 at 19:11
12 people like this

Dottie Harris is thinking a cardboard box rocket with a blanket roof is rather hot work on a sunny day.
August 10, 2012 at 11:21
3 people like this

Dottie Harris didn't realise how quickly wax crayons melted in a conservatory before she sat on a ready melted one in her new dress.
August 10, 2012 at 15:01
4 people like this

Dottie Harris is witnessing a particularly bad case of man flu. The Monster "can't walk" as his "whole body hurts." THREE insect bites are the cause. Give. Me. Strength.
August 13, 2012 at 11:01
7 people like this

Dottie Harris thinks that when she says to The Monster "Flush the toilet, please" she does not want the response to be "NO, YOU DO IT OR I WILL PUT YOU IN IT." Bar is open.
August 13, 2012 at 19:08
4 people like this

Dottie Harris is slightly embarrassed she's the only parent at crazy golf who not only requested a score card but is keeping actual score.
August 14, 2012 at 14:23
13 people like this

Dottie Harris is having a cup of tea. She's in bed, it's still hot, it's quiet and nobody has dribbled milk into her nose. Thanks, Mum. x

August 17, 2012 at 7:54

9 people like this

Dottie Harris is hiding in the kitchen "putting stuff away" to avoid a sandy bath time after a lovely day at the beach!

August 18, 2012 at 18:43

6 people like this

Dottie Harris is still unconvinced by yellow nail varnish.

August 18, 2012 at 20:21

3 people like this

Dottie Harris dislikes Mondays. High (low) point so far is being stuck on top of a chest of drawers as the stool used to get up there is now being used as a birthday cake. Having to blow out the candles and eat the cake to get down was the final straw. Send gin!

August 20, 2012 at 9:53

16 people like this

Dottie Harris has never seen anybody carry a sword in a flowery shopping bag, but according to The Monster that's how it's done.

August 24, 2012 at 15:08

5 people like this

Dottie Harris is glad her daughter felt the need to get up and shout at her 6 times last night. After all, too much sleep makes for a lazy Mummy.
Sob

August 25, 2012 at 7:25

3 people like this

Dottie Harris really wishes she hadn't discovered *24* on Netflix. ADDICT.
August 26, 2012 at 23:51
10 people like this

Dottie Harris thinks that you know it's been a busy Bank Holiday when you end up with two sobbing kids in the bath. Time for gin and potentially more melted cheese.
August 27, 2012 at 19:13
9 people like this

Dottie Harris really wishes Lego police vans didn't hurt so much when driven over her face at 6:30 a.m.
August 28, 2012 at 6:48
6 people like this

Dottie Harris just nipped upstairs after tucking the kids into bed, and has discovered The Chubster in the lounge flicking through the TV channels. Locks on doors are OK, yes?
August 28, 2012 at 19:23
11 people like this

Dottie Harris isn't thinking about the two slices of cherry pie in the fridge. Especially NOT when they could be teamed with a hot chocolate.
August 29, 2012 at 11:02
4 people like this

Dottie Harris is very pleased that when she asked The Chubster what she wanted to do this afternoon she said go shopping for home furnishings and storage solutions. *Cough*
September 1, 2012 at 14:54
6 people like this

Dottie Harris is amazed how warm croissants and a pot
of tea make everything alright. Except for the fact that
she is now obviously 70 years old.
September 2, 2012 at 8:19
5 people like this

Dottie Harris was meant to be practicing the whole
"getting up on time for school" thing today. She failed.
September 3, 2012 at 8:47
2 people like this

Dottie Harris has just heard The Monster say "Stop
being a naughty scoundrel" to Batman. As you do.
September 3, 2012 at 10:12
7 people like this

Dottie Harris - Day 2 of attempting practice. Husband
says "What? I have to get up at 7 a.m. as well?" There are
no words.
September 4, 2012 at 7:03
3 people like this

Dottie Harris has dropped her big boy at school.
Wahhh
September 5, 2012 at 9:14
19 people like this

Dottie Harris is pleased to report that The Monster had
an amazing day, has been "excellent" and is "so well
behaved." He also wasn't that filthy!
September 5, 2012 at 16:08
27 people like this

Dottie Harris thinks The Monster has left his "he's SOOO good and cute" personality at school with the doting teacher and has brought the "he's a horrible little toad" one home with him. Send help!
September 6, 2012 at 15:54
4 people like this

Dottie Harris *must* remember to wash school uniforms.
September 9, 2012 at 18:39
2 people like this

Dottie Harris is wondering at what age it's feasible to suggest The Monster gets himself up, ready and off to school.
September 10, 2012 at 6:34
9 people like this

Dottie Harris is baffled by the skill of a child who hates fruit and veg. Eating all the omelette and not a bite of peppers.
September 10, 2012 at 12:26
5 people like this

Dottie Harris is disappointed that her change of hair cut and colour didn't disguise her enough to stop the teachers sending the children home with her.
September 11, 2012 at 16:01
6 people like this

Dottie Harris was slightly embarrassed explaining to his teachers that the reason The Monster didn't want to come into school today was because it "is boring."
September 12, 2012 at 9:08
5 people like this

Dottie Harris is amazed it took as long as a week for the big blue eyes to work. The Monster has convinced his teachers that he needs to be fed his dinner at lunch time, rather than feeding himself. Well, according to him anyway.

September 12, 2012 at 17:25

2 people like this

Dottie Harris - Two phrases I never thought I'd say: "We don't put buses on people's heads" and "No, the laptop isn't a dog" (as it's dragged across the landing by its USB cable). Send gin.

September 13, 2012 at 11:47

11 people like this

Dottie Harris is very pleased her daughter tried to help her by hanging the laundry on the radiators, she just wishes it wasn't the dirty laundry.

September 13, 2012 at 17:12

6 people like this

Dottie Harris is becoming an expert at attending superhero parties. Perhaps it's time to purchase a She-Ra outfit.

September 14, 2012 at 14:57

9 people like this

Dottie Harris slightly resents sharing her cooked breakfast with the fat child who kept her awake between 12:30 a.m. and 4:30 a.m.

September 15, 2012 at 8:27

1 person likes this

Dottie Harris loves that her husband ordered her a curry WITHOUT looking for a voucher because he knows just how horrible her day has been. Now that's love.
September 15, 2012 at 20:01
16 people like this

Dottie Harris thinks you know it's not going to be a good nappy situation when you stand in poo that has obviously escaped from said nappy.
September 16, 2012 at 17:59
9 people like this

Dottie Harris could be mistaken as a domestic goddess after her morning in the kitchen. However, if you'd look around the corner where The Chubster had been "quietly playing" you'd have found all the dust, fluff and odd socks she'd been fishing out from under the sofa. Just to confirm, we quietly pushed them all back under again for another day.
September 17, 2012 at 11:58
3 people like this

Dottie Harris has just witnessed her daughter trying to take the easel and chalk box to bed.
September 17, 2012 at 19:16
6 people like this

Dottie Harris has invented a new drinking game. Every time she has to split up a fight she takes a shot. Every time she has to tell The Monster not to answer back she takes a shot and every time she has to tell The Chubster to stop climbing the stair gate she takes a shot. Let's hope nobody has a breathalyser at the school gates as we've not even had breakfast yet and she's nearly drunk.
September 18, 2012 at 7:59
5 people like this

Dottie Harris must not go to the gym before having to look after her children on her own. Dealing with a nose bleed when barely able to walk is not easy.
September 18, 2012 at 17:01
3 people like this

Dottie Harris is not enjoying the cold.
September 20, 2012 at 8:55
2 people like this

Dottie Harris has discovered The Chubster taking a shape sorter and a baby walker to bed.
September 20, 2012 at 19:34
9 people like this

Dottie Harris is putting her children out with the charity bags.
September 21, 2012 at 7:01
6 people like this

Dottie Harris thinks it may have taken 57 minutes, 23 treks upstairs, confiscation of a fire engine, a bus, a doll, an entire HappyLand toy box, 3 books, a pull-along phone and 4 dummies (1 in the mouth, 2 in the eye and 1 "just in case") but The Chubster MAY have finally gone down for a nap.
September 21, 2012 at 14:21
19 people like this

Dottie Harris spoke too soon.
September 21, 2012 at 14:23
7 people like this

Dottie Harris never thought she'd be grateful for 3 hours of solid sleep, but she is.
September 22, 2012 at 6:48
2 people like this

Dottie Harris is losing the "Let's have a third takeaway this week" battle.
September 23, 2012 at 19:13
4 people like this

Dottie Harris shouldn't have pressed the snooze button.
September 26, 2012 at 7:28
6 people like this

Dottie Harris - Fail of working for yourself from home: Having to work in the evening due to general family chaos. Bonus of working for yourself from home (in the evening): gin.
September 26, 2012 at 20:09
9 people like this

Dottie Harris has just been told by The Monster that he "blooming well will have cake for tea." Hmm.
September 27, 2012 at 16:47
11 people like this

Dottie Harris is witnessing a tantrum from hell because she put *The Gruffalo's Child* on instead of *The Gruffalo*. Somebody is a *tad* touchy today!
September 28, 2012 at 17:01
3 people like this

Dottie Harris has just received a tirade of abuse for giving The Chubster a smoothie.
September 29, 2012 at 10:11
11 people like this

Dottie Harris had a feeling it was going to be a tough morning when the first thing she heard was "Mmmuuummmmmyyyy SHE is POINTING at me."
October 1, 2012 at 11:21
9 people like this

Dottie Harris, after blood, sweat and tears, has achieved an *Alice in Wonderland* playing card costume for school on Friday, only to be informed by The Monster that actually it's rather rubbish and he wants to be the Cheshire Cat. Er. No.
October 2, 2012 at 16:23
4 people like this

Dottie Harris thinks The Chubster's landing meltdown is hindering her Friday night gin consumption.
October 5, 2012 at 19:38
7 people like this

Dottie Harris thinks her husband will be owing her a present for deleting *The X Factor* so he could record the Formula 1. You know, the Formula 1 that is on now while she's awake and he's asleep. She's thinking a car would be nice.
October 7, 2012 at 8:03
12 people like this

Dottie Harris just had a VERY productive couple of hours at the gym.
Ahem JacuzziAndSaunaAndGossiping *Ahem*
October 7, 2012 at 14:58
3 people like this

Dottie Harris had a wholesome lunch of beef Hula Hoops followed by 6 Rich Tea biscuits. Classy.
October 8, 2012 at 13:41
2 people like this

Dottie Harris thinks that next parents' evening she may be relegated to end of the line when her 10- minute slot turned into 25 minutes. *Ahem* She just likes to get all the details. Plus she was giving the teacher a chance to use the word GENIUS. She didn't.
October 10, 2012 at 21:01
19 people like this

Dottie Harris woke up at 10 a.m. and had a cup of tea in bed. Just saying.
October 13, 2012 at 11:01
3 people like this

Dottie Harris had a FAB sneaky night away with him indoors, but is very happy to be back in her little house with her beautiful little monkeys (now that they're asleep).
October 13, 2012 at 19:37
2 people like this

Dottie Harris wonders if the teaching assistant who would happily take The Monster home would be happy just collecting him and taking him to school every day instead. Cold.
October 15, 2012 at 6:58
5 people like this

Dottie Harris wonders if stealing the last Haribo is grounds for divorcing a greedy husband?
October 16, 2012 at 20:46
7 people like this

Dottie Harris is unsure how she is going to attempt, let alone maintain, a glam mum image on the school run today. The only fashion statement may be drowned rat.
October 17, 2012 at 8:19
9 people like this

Dottie Harris wonders how two small children can cause so much brain ache in such a short amount of time. Bar is open. Pass the gin.
Sob
October 17, 2012 at 19:01
16 people like this

Dottie Harris is currently listening to The Chubster empty the bookcase and The Monster bellowing "SHUT UP YOU'RE GIVING ME A HEADACHE." Ironic.
October 18, 2012 at 19:13
9 people like this

Dottie Harris was informed by nursery school today that her daughter was so cross about having to leave the "garden centre" play area for group time that she stuck her head in a bucket of compost.
October 19, 2012 at 17:56
29 people like this

Dottie Harris thinks it's slightly unfair that her daughter doesn't want Mummy to have a pair of Kensington Ugg Boots for her second birthday. SELFISH.
October 20, 2012 at 7:38
5 people like this

Dottie Harris is wishing she'd never taught The Monster the word "compromise."
October 22, 2012 at 8:15
12 people like this

Dottie Harris - The Chubster's opinion of healthy banana muffins: Look at them, laugh and crumble them on the floor.
October 23, 2012 at 8:09
4 people like this

Dottie Harris can't believe her baby is 2! Happy Birthday Chubs! xxxx
October 25, 2012 at 7:01
24 people like this

Dottie Harris is on the way to Peppa Pig World wondering if she'll make it through the car journey. Send gin.
October 26, 2012 at 7:27
5 people like this

Dottie Harris didn't enjoy having to clear sick out of the car in the hail just now. Poor Monster. :(
October 27, 2012 at 15:45
7 people like this

Dottie Harris loves her children with all her heart. However, she really wishes they had mute and pause buttons.
October 28, 2012 at 8:01
6 people like this

Dottie Harris can't believe her son can unlock the bathroom door with a 10p piece.
October 29, 2012 at 10:08
11 people like this

Dottie Harris - Bedtime battle: Mummy 1 - Chubs 0.
October 30, 2012 at 7:01
6 people like this

Dottie Harris - HA: 2-0
October 31, 2012 at 7:15
8 people like this

Dottie Harris would like to remind all teenage trick-or-treaters that a mask (that you don't even put over your face) and a bike do not make a costume.
October 31, 2012 at 18:57
4 people like this

Dottie Harris may or may not have ignored the doorbell so she could eat the leftover Haribo.
October 31, 2012 at 19:34
6 people like this

Dottie Harris has just seen her daughter take yesterday's half-eaten mini roll out of the bin and eat it.
November 2, 2012 at 16:11
9 people like this

Dottie Harris has finished watching *Ghostwatch* and therefore has no chance of sleep, especially after The Chubster dropped her cup out of bed at a critical pipe banging scene.
November 4, 2012 at 22:56
12 people like this

Dottie Harris is quickly losing the will to live.
November 5, 2012 at 18:34
6 people like this

Dottie Harris genuinely doesn't know if she'll make it through the day now that she's run out of Rich Tea biscuits.
November 6, 2012 at 11:32
5 people like this

Dottie Harris has just been asked by a 4-year-old if she's *actually* an adult. She's assuming the response "Go back to blinking sleep" doesn't back up her case.
November 6, 2012 at 20:01
6 people like this

Dottie Harris wants to apologise to the doctor for being told by a 4-year-old that she's "a bit rubbish" because she didn't produce and apply eczema cream then and there in the surgery.
November 7, 2012 at 15:28
6 people like this

Dottie Harris is struggling to help her son complete his homework. JUST WRITE THE LETTER "S," THAT'S ALL YOU NEED TO DO!
November 7, 2012 at 17:32
5 people like this

Dottie Harris will not be attempting the school run without the pushchair again. Tantrum a go-go.
November 9, 2012 at 9:23
9 people like this

Dottie Harris - Sleep! LOTS OF SLEEP!
November 10, 2012 at 7:24
5 people like this

Dottie Harris is still singing the Jolly Phonics songs to herself even though she's on her own. "The snake is in the grassss, the snake is in the grasss..."
November 13, 2012 at 10:01
6 people like this

Dottie Harris wasn't embarrassed at all at her daughter's refusal to leave nursery school. Or the fact that she had to sit on her to put her coat on. Or the fact that she was kicked and hit in the face. Or the fact that they had to be escorted to the car park. Pass the gin.
November 13, 2012 at 18:59
17 people like this

Dottie Harris is glad she bothered to make The Monster a spotty T-shirt for *Children in Need*. Especially as his response was "But I wantttteeedddd sppoootttyyyyyy trroouussseeerrrssss."
Whimper
November 15, 2012 at 16:28
6 people like this

Dottie Harris may have three dresses that all look perfectly lovely, but in true form has nothing to wear.
November 16, 2012 at 19:03
5 people like this

Dottie Harris thinks building a pirate ship straight after painting her nails was a mistake.
November 17, 2012 at 15:21
9 people like this

Dottie Harris is pooped. One night out and she's considering bringing the jimjams out before 5 p.m.!
November 18, 2012 at 16:21
3 people like this

Dottie Harris and The Chubster have just demolished a pack of Jaffa Cakes. On Chubs' insistence, obviously.
Cough
November 20, 2012 at 11:41
2 people like this

Dottie Harris is pleased to hear from The Monster that Daddy has "loads of money for presents this Christmas." Diamonds it is then!
November 20, 2012 at 19:01

9 people like this

Dottie Harris thinks it's true love. Husband has bought her ice cube trays shaped like stars because she was grumpy they only had square ones. Little things.
November 20, 2012 at 19:28

6 people like this

Dottie Harris really wishes her daughter would draw on the furniture she's trying to replace rather than the nice stuff.
November 22, 2012 at 11:42

5 people like this

Dottie Harris wants to thank Lincolnshire Police for being so understanding about The Chubster's 999 call earlier.
November 23, 2012 at 14:25

19 people like this

Dottie Harris wonders how she's going to bribe The Monster after the 25th of December.
November 27, 2012 at 16:26

10 people like this

Dottie Harris is feeling really, really tired.
November 28, 2012 at 15:08

3 people like this

Dottie Harris is drowning in a 4-year-old's homework.
November 29, 2012 at 16:21

6 people like this

Dottie Harris has discovered she is quite a sore loser when it comes to school raffles.
November 30, 2012 at 18:24
6 people like this

Dottie Harris isn't the only person to tell her children that Santa lives in the house alarm sensor, along with the Easter Bunny and Tooth Fairy, is she?
December 2, 2012 at 9:31
17 people like this

Dottie Harris is unsure how to deal with the fact that The Chubster is scared of Advent calendars.
December 3, 2012 at 7:01
5 people like this

Dottie Harris has not only had another "DOES" "DOESN'T" "DOES" "DOESN'T" argument with The Monster, but it was followed by "I'M NEVER TALKING TO YOU AGAIN. YOU'RE NOT MY BEST FRIEND ANY MORE." Perhaps saying "Thank God, do you promise?" wasn't the response he was expecting.
December 3, 2012 at 18:59
4 people like this

Dottie Harris is slightly baffled as to how The Chubster has managed to come home from nursery school with only one sock on.
December 4, 2012 at 18:32
2 people like this

Dottie Harris - The Monster on *The Snowman*: "That's stupid. You can't walk on the air, only fly."
December 5, 2012 at 16:23
16 people like this

Dottie Harris really wants a bowl of Coco Pops for dinner, but apparently that's not "nutritious."
December 5, 2012 at 20:04
6 people like this

Dottie Harris - HE'S TRAINED!!! On our 9th wedding anniversary, he finally brings me a cup of tea without being asked.
December 6, 2012 at 7:01
9 people like this

Dottie Harris may never speak to her son again. Mariah's "All I Want for Christmas" is NOT the "rubbish-est song ever."
December 7, 2012 at 16:23
6 people like this

Dottie Harris has just gained 40 pounds looking at her Christmas food shopping list and can't wait to get stuck in.
December 9, 2012 at 21:04
7 people like this

Dottie Harris thinks it was totally worth paying to have the carpet cleaned just to have The Chubster wee all over it less than 24 hours later.
December 11, 2012 at 9:01
8 people like this

Dottie Harris totally managed to stop the tears (snot) at The Monster's first school nativity. It was close though!
December 13, 2012 at 11:43
6 people like this

Dottie Harris - Watching a 4-year-old write Christmas cards? Most. Painful. Experience. Ever.
December 13, 2012 at 16:29
16 people like this

Dottie Harris - Gin.
December 13, 2012 at 17:03
12 people like this

Dottie Harris - Strange thing #987 Chubs is scared of: the squirrel in *Ice Age*. *Ice Age* is now playing as payback for her earlier meltdown. Karma.
December 14, 2012 at 11:45
9 people like this

Dottie Harris is having a sofa day with poorly Monster. She's not feeling too bright herself if she's honest.
December 17, 2012 at 9:12
6 people like this

Dottie Harris is thinking that The Chubster climbing out of her high chair and crawling across the table is perhaps the final straw for the day. Two hours until they're in bed.
December 17, 2012 at 17:03
4 people like this

Dottie Harris has just completed "emergency crafting." She's sure nursery school should have made the party hats for us.
December 17, 2012 at 23:12
6 people like this

Dottie Harris is perhaps a little emotional today. A child pushed Chubs at nursery school, and she's not sure who cried more.
December 19, 2012 at 19:01
8 people like this

Dottie Harris - Not great weather for PJ day at school.
December 20, 2012 at 8:55
3 people like this

Dottie Harris thinks that whilst it's lovely her husband has finished work for the holidays, she hasn't, and she's not interested in watching *Jeremy Kyle* right now, thank you very much.
December 20, 2012 at 9:28
9 people like this

Dottie Harris - Words you don't expect to be greeted with when returning from the supermarket: "Take this bag; it's dripping poo juice."
December 20, 2012 at 18:57
4 people like this

Dottie Harris is hiding in the en-suite with a box of Quality Street waiting for bath time to be over.
December 21, 2012 at 18:14
6 people like this

Dottie Harris thinks that whilst The Chubster's pretend snoring is very cute, she would like it more if she didn't do it so close to her face.
December 22, 2012 at 6:58
4 people like this

Dottie Harris knows when you have to call Santa from the breakfast table it's going to be One of Those Days.
December 22, 2012 at 8:43
11 people like this

Dottie Harris would like to apologise to the woman at the soft play whose bottom Chubs felt the need to constantly squeeze. With both hands.
December 22, 2012 at 16:21
6 people like this

Dottie Harris - Present wrapping and Jazz FM. That's how cool she is these days.
December 23, 2012 at 21:03
3 people like this

Dottie Harris is waiting for The Monster to wake up. Merry Christmas, folks. x
December 25, 2012 at 6:01
7 people like this

Dottie Harris might have to start opening The Monster's presents soon if he doesn't JUST WAKE UP!!!!
December 25, 2012 at 7:38
9 people like this

Dottie Harris - The irony! Chubs liking FRUIT cake.
December 26, 2012 at 14:23
4 people like this

Dottie Harris is so pleased she suggested a digital camera for The Monster for Christmas. Note to self: Lock door when showering.
Sigh
December 30, 2012 at 9:34
15 people like this

Dottie Harris is coming to terms with the fact that Chubs is not a genius and the reason she can count backwards may be something to do with the Louis Spence "Go Compare" advert. Oh.

December 30, 2012 at 10:08

5 people like this

Dottie Harris - Before everything gets clogged up, Happy New Year, folks. P.S. 2013 is the year I FINALLY get my 4x4. There's another Harris on the way...

December 31, 2012 at 23:53

43 people like this

acknowledgements

First and foremost, I have to thank Matthew. He is full of encouragement and support, and ends up fairly battered after each writing experience. He refuses to read anything in fear of saying the wrong thing.

And it's only fair to thank the Internet. In particular Twitter and Facebook. Without the encouragement and support of social media, Dottie wouldn't be here today. Who'd have thought my little project would have turned into something I'm so proud of? To those in the writing groups on Facebook who take the time to support each other, thank you. Plus a special shout out to Kerry, who probably feels like she's on 24/7 support watch.

Mum, thank you for teaching me to believe in myself. I forget it most days, but the mantra of "you can do anything you want if you try" has been drilled into me, and for that I will always be grateful.

Theo and Larry, without you I'd still think motherhood and being a grown up was all white linen trousers and Boden raincoats.

To everyone who bought the book first time around, if you're reading this you've bought it again, so thank you!

Finally, thank you to Adria, Vicki and everyone else at Velvet Morning Press for making the first part of my dream come true.

aBOUT THe auTHOr

Aimee is from Lincoln, England, where she enjoys drinking gin and spending time with her family (and she won't tell you which of those she prefers doing). As a child, one of her favourite parts of the summer holidays was to devour all the books in a little book shop in Devon. She continued reading at lightning speed right up until having children. She now reads with eyes propped open by match sticks.

Aimee hopes you enjoyed the book! If you did, she'd love it if you left a review at Amazon. For every review—even just a few sentences—Amazon sends Aimee a bottle of gin. OK, not really. But Amazon does help convince other people to buy Aimee's book, which is arguably even better. Depending on the brand of gin.

Want more? Get *Lush in Translation* for free! Simply join Aimee's mailing list: http://eepurl.com/qSk_f.

Check out the full Survival Series, featuring Dottie Harris:

Survival of the Ginnest, a modern-day diary of a new mom.

Survival of the Christmas Spirit, a humorous short story about Dottie's Christmas gone horribly wrong.

Mothers Ruined, a funny novel of Dottie's misadventures in suburbia.

Lush in Translation, a funny short story highlighting the differences between the British and Americans.

For more about Aimee, check out PassTheGin.co.uk. And you can always drop Aimee a line at mrs@aimee-horton.co.uk.

Read on for a sneak peek of *Mothers Ruined*, slated for release in Autumn 2015...

Find out just how British Dottie is in...
Lush in Translation

Dottie Harris is as British as they come, which is exactly what endears her to us. But when her pregnant American cousin comes for a visit, Dottie is a frazzled disaster who can't seem to overcome the language barrier.

Lush in Translation is a funny look at parenting from both sides of the pond, and the surprising number of confusing language differences that entails.

Get it for free! Join Aimee's new release mailing list and she'll send you a free ecopy of *Lush in Translation*: http://eepurl.com/qSk_f.

MOTHERS RUINED

1.

aM I THe ONLY ONe WHOSe PLaNS aLWaYS GO WrONG?

WHY THE HELL IS HE NOT PICKING UP HIS PHONE?

I'm driving really fast. Well as fast as you can when you're stuck behind a tractor going less than 20 miles an hour, on what feels like a single track road. There can't possibly be enough room to overtake, even though that really big posh looking car has just overtaken us both and appears to already be just a speck in the distance.

I glance at the seat next to me, where a Tesco carrier bag stuffed with various snacks, fruit shoots and about five different electrical gadgets is resting, along with my hospital bag. By hospital bag, I mean random clothes rammed into the first handbag I could find that didn't have a thin layer of mini-cheddar crumbs crushed into the lining.

I didn't expect this baby for another three or four weeks. How the hell was I supposed to know it would bloody come early?

The nearly out-of-battery iPad is charging on the phone charger plugged into what used to be a cigarette lighter, and my mobile is propped precariously on the dashboard in front of the petrol gauge. Stabbing at the screen again, I select Henry's number for what feels like the 100th time, and listen to it ring out. The kids in the back are irritating me even more by counting how many rings it does before it goes to voice mail. This time it only does three before the sound of Henry's "grown-up work voice" comes out of the tinny speakerphone and informs me he's away on business and will be back in the office next week.

He's bloody diverted my call! Three rings means he's seen my name and diverted it! The idiot.

Pulling the car over, I grab my phone and Google Henry's Scotland office. A place he visits every few months yet I've never needed to call, always relying on his mobile phone to get in contact. However, this time it's serious.

"I need to talk to Henry Harris please," I say to the Scottish voice on the other end of the phone, attempting to sound calm, even though I can feel a niggling pain start again in my lower back. The receptionist begins to inform me he's in a meeting right now, but with the cars racing past and the kids shouting I can't hear her, and I lose patience.

"Look, can you give him an urgent message… no… I don't want him to call me back, I need you to use these exact words: THE BABY IS COMING GET YOUR BLOODY ARSE HOME NOW. Have you got that?"

It's times like this I wish I could slam my phone down instead of just pressing the screen angrily.

The pain begins to subside, and I try not to think about how cross Henry is going to be with me for speaking to her like that.

I suppose it was a bit rude.

But I'm having a bloody baby!

It's not enough that he pissed off on a jolly to drink whisky for nearly a week and left me to move house on my own with the two kids—oh no. Now he's going to miss the birth of his third bloody child, his second daughter. And yet again I'm left to do everything myself. I can't do it all. I mean, I can't even work out how to use the bloody newfangled baby monitor. It just keeps screeching white noise at me or playing some random music.

Starting the engine, I take a deep breath and carry on to the hospital. But all I can think about is how if I can't manage to turn on a baby monitor, how can I look after three children on my own?

Arriving at the hospital, I reach into my bag for my wallet, but I can't find it. Shit! How am I going to buy a parking ticket? I continue to rummage about, but as I work my way through button-down nighties, big pants and feeding bras, the image of my lovely tan and pink leather wallet flashes in front of my eyes. It's next to the kettle.

How the hell did I forget my wallet? I NEVER forget my wallet. You never know when there's going to be a good shopping opportunity.

Sod it, I don't have time to worry about little things like parking tickets. Balancing a vile-smelling, nearly asleep Mabel on my hip, I grab Arthur's hand and make my way towards the entrance of the maternity wing. I'm nearly at the door when I hear a shout, and turning around, I see the traffic warden waving his hand at me to indicate my ticketless car.

This isn't fair. Why do they charge for parking anyway?

In a sudden burst of pain-free energy, still gripping my bag and the kids, I march back towards him. As I approach my car, I realise he's actually writing me a ticket—he's not even given me a chance!

"You going inside to get change for the machine?" he

asks, not even looking at me. He holds the ticket in the air, in what I can only assume is an overly dramatic way of giving me one last chance to say I was going to get change. But of course I don't give him that answer. Instead I squeeze between my car and the one parked next to it and snatch the ticket off him.

"I…" I begin, through gritted teeth as another pain builds up. "Am… in… bloody… labour…" He opens his mouth, starting to say something as he reaches forward, attempting to take his ticket back. And that's when it hurts. Like proper hurts, and before I drop her, I thrust Mabel at him and grip the bonnet of the car, letting go of Arthur's hand and the parking ticket as I do. The traffic warden visibly recoils, and I'm not entirely sure whether it's because of the smell coming from Mabel, who is wriggling in his arms, or because the ticket flies into the air and is carried away by the breeze.

Where the hell is Henry? How the heck am I meant to deal with all this on my own?

"Let's get you inside, Miss." I hear the attendant's gruff voice, and holding onto the kids, he ushers me forwards. As we approach, we see a big sign on the automatic door. It reads "DOORS BROKEN, PLEASE USE REVOLVING DOOR" in bright red letters. The man moves through first, holding Arthur's hand and Mabel in his arms.

Through the glass, I can see a look of panic forming on Mabel's face as she leaves me outside. Not wanting her to be scared at a time like this—I'm already terrified—I hurriedly move towards the door to follow them, looking down at my stomach.

"Whose bright idea was it to put a revolving door in a maternity wing anyway?" I mutter. Taking a deep breath, I give the door a shove. It moves quickly, quicker than I thought, and one of the sections passes me by, then another. In a panic, I try and jump into the next, managing to squeeze into the tiny compartment. I give another little push hoping it will move round just as quickly, but realise my bag is preventing it from moving.

Shuffling in farther, I drop my bag to the floor between my feet and try again. Nothing. My bump is too big; I can't get the right angle. Damn it! I can hear Mabel calling my name. Her voice is on edge, and she could start screaming any minute now.

For crying out loud.

I turn sideways so that my bump is facing the middle, then take a step to the side. This time the door moves, and I manage to slowly sidestep round until a draft of air-conditioned air hits my red cheeks and the back of my neck. Collapsing into an undignified squat, I scoop up my bag before straightening up, and turn around so I can make my way into the hospital. But as I do, my bump knocks the door, making it move again.

I back out of the door slowly, shuffling so as not to trip over myself or any other unseen obstacle. Finally both feet hit the pale pink vinyl floor, and I turn around just in time to see two young nurses and the car park attendant looking at me and trying not to laugh.

With as much dignity as I can muster, I raise my arm to wave at them, but in doing so I manage to clout myself in the face. Instead of trying to save my dignity any further, I turn to the kids and point to some chairs next to a big television.

"Artie… here are some crisps for you, and Mabel, go and sit on those seats over there while Mummy talks to the nice midwife," I say, collapsing into a wheelchair next to me, nearly knocking another pregnant woman over as she is about to ease herself into it. She opens her mouth, ready to say something, but I silence her with a glare.

That's when I realise how serious the situation really is, because while Henry will probably miss the birth of his child, the two small children already halfway through a bag of Pom-Bears might not.

I need a gin and tonic.

"Something's not right."

The words ring in my ears, and my exhausted, aching body jumps to attention.

After I collapsed in the wheelchair, the kids were ushered off with a nice nurse, and I was wheeled in for an examination. I was only two centimeters dilated.

How the hell can I be only two centimeters dilated? I thought I was at least eight!

It feels like I've been here for days. They started to make noises about sending me home, muttering things about "coming back in a few hours," but I couldn't stand it. I could feel my voice getting higher and higher as I told them how hard it had been to get here. I told them how my waters had broken on the stairs after celebrating a successful poo in the toilet (Mabel not me). I told them how I'd assumed it was a huge wee, but then the pains kept coming and coming all through the afternoon and the school run. That's when they changed their minds and whisked me off for another examination, promising me the kids were perfectly happy and that they would try to find out where Henry was.

That was hours ago, and now here I am with those terrifying three words hanging in the air and ringing in my ears.

Something's not right.

"What's not right?" I ask, but it comes out as a whisper. Not that anybody is listening to me anyway. In fact, they're all whispering to each other. I turn to the midwife hovering next to me, but she avoids eye contact.

"What's not right?" I say again, louder. I can hear the fear in my voice.

"Right, baby seems to be in a bit of an awkward

position," she trills, patting my hand. "We're just fetching the consultant to come and have a look." She is smiling and seems perfectly calm, but I can't get the words "something's not right" out of my head.

What am I going to do? How can I be doing this on my own?

That's when I remember Jane. My best friend Jane works on the children's ward. As soon as her name pops into my mind, I start to breathe properly again. She's at work today! Right at this very moment she is somewhere in this very hospital.

She'll know what to do.

In my excitement, I gabble at the midwife, who eventually understands what I'm trying to say, and they put out a page.

As we're waiting for Jane to appear, a doctor walks in. He's tall, dark and looks to be in his late 50s. He obviously recognises me, but I don't have a clue who he is.

"Dottie Harris! I thought you were never going to have another baby as long as you lived!" His eyes are sparkling, and he has a smile on his face.

He must have been here when one of the kids was born.

"How is the young man?" he asks as he examines me. I start to tell him about Arthur and now Mabel, but he stands up and cuts me off. "This baby looks like it's going to be a monkey, breech, so we need to start thinking about other options."

What does that mean? I can't cope with this.

Totally overwhelmed, I burst into tears. Just then, Jane comes running into the room, closely followed by a midwife who informs me that while she's not been able to get through to Henry directly, his office has confirmed he's on his way.

On his bloody way? If he hadn't gone to bloody Scotland he'd be here by now, telling me everything is going to be OK. Luckily I have Jane.

Jane is already by my side, stroking my hair and holding my hand. After a few reassuring words, she turns to the doctor and asks, in a calm and composed voice, what my options are.

Jane talks me through what the doctor said, and I look at her blankly. Soon she realises I'm too far gone to hear anything in detail so pauses for a moment. "They were going to try and turn the baby manually, but it's too late for that now. So you're more than likely going to have a C-section." Her blue eyes are full of concern, and she searches my face, waiting for my reaction.

The words hit me like a punch in the stomach. Either that or it's another contraction. I irrationally blame Henry for all that's gone wrong.

Idiot husband. If we'd not bought that stupid house, I'd not had to start bloody decorating the bloody awful nursery and gone into labour. If it wasn't for him I wouldn't bloody be here now. Alone.

Just as I start ranting at Jane, the door flings open again, and we all turn to stare. A midwife shouts, "Sir… sir… please who are you?!" and Henry appears at the door, closely followed by two security guards in hot pursuit. As soon as they see me half-lying, half-sitting on a hospital bed, my legs akimbo and my gown hitched up around my knees, they stop short. One turns a funny shade of green, and looking at his shoes, starts to whistle tunelessly.

Yeah, because he's the one in the awkward position… but wait, Henry is here?

"HENRY!" I cry, and the tears start pouring down my face again as he runs towards me and grabs my other hand.

"I told you I'd be here!" He smiles down at me before winking at Jane who tactfully lets go and leaves the room.

I want to punch him, and I actually clench my fist, but another pain comes. Instead I satisfy myself with squeezing his hand extra tight, making sure my engagement ring digs really hard into him. To give him his dues, he doesn't even cry out in pain, although I kind of wish he had.

"How did you get here? It takes hours to drive from Scotland," I say when the pain passes. "I haven't been here that long have I?" I look around, disorientated.

"I flew. Jumped on the first plane here," he says, grinning as he wipes my face and squeezes my snotty nose with a tissue. I feel a warm flush of pride grow on my cheeks. But wait a minute, this is Henry.

"You FLEW?" I cry, unable to keep the disbelief from my voice. Henry would never pay for a direct flight; he won't even pay for the train unless it's on expenses.

Am I dreaming? Am I already in theatre? Have I died?

Laughing, he kisses my forehead and shrugs his shoulders. "So, what's happened? Where are we now?"

"Well, I got stuck in the door on the way in after the stupid car park attendant tried to give me a ticket, and I thought the removal men had tried to kidnap Mabel, but I found her hiding in a cupboard, and the nursery is all painted. I painted it pink and was just about to pull the carpet up, but then Mabel did a poo in the toilet... and that's when I think it all started. My waters broke on the stairs—don't worry, I cleaned it up—but then Mabel threw up on the slide in the school playground and slid through it, she stinks, and I forgot to put the washing in the dryer, and oh God. I was so rude to the girl at your office, I'm sorry I was just so scared and... oh... shit that hurts." I gabble, and as another pain surges through me and snot bubbles come out of my nose, I grab his arm and wipe my nose and cheek with his suit jacket.

"Shhh," he says, pushing my hair away from my face. Then, turning to the midwife who is standing nearby, he murmurs, "Is she delirious?"

Before she has a chance to answer, the consultant is

back in the room, and after a quick examination, he announces the baby is in distress.

No, I don't want her to be in distress!

He begins to fire out instructions to the room, which is suddenly full of people. He turns to me and Henry, telling us I have to go into surgery now, that it's not too late and that I can have an epidural. Then he turns to Henry, who is gripping my hand, and I can tell he's trying to stay calm for me but he's gone a bit pale and keeps clearing his throat. He clears it so often I don't catch everything the consultant is telling him—something about where he needs to go while I'm going through to theatre?

Everything is happening so fast, and I'm terrified. I'm being wheeled off, and Henry is left on his own. I hear him shout, "I LOVE YOU!"

"Please don't put me to sleep! I'm not ready to die yet! I want Henry... HENRY!" I cry all over again, and the midwife comes to calm me down. Holding my hand, she bends down next to me.

"Dottie," she says. "Now Dottie, listen to me. You aren't going to sleep. We're keeping you awake. Remember, you had an epidural with Mabel, didn't you?" She's gripping my hand and speaking firmly. "Henry can come in as soon as he's scrubbed up, but we have to get to work now. He or she is in distress, so the sooner they're out, the better. Do you understand?"

Nodding my head slightly, I say, "She. It's a girl. I want to name her Martha, but Henry doesn't think having 'two Ms' is a good idea." I feel my breathing return to normal as I say, "Maybe after going through *this*, I can persuade him." I said it more to myself than anyone else, but the midwife laughs, and I'm sure she just rolled her eyes. She continues to hold my hand, more gently, as the anesthetist explains what's going to happen.

By the time the needle has been inserted (it takes three attempts as I'm shaking so much), Henry is by my side and holding my hand. Together, we wait expectantly.

I have no idea what's going on. I stare at the ceiling, at the blue screen constructed by a sheet, trying to work out what's happening. Henry looks a bit green, but keeps looking at me reassuringly, smiling and nodding as if everything's OK.

After what seems like ages, there is a bit of a kerfuffle, then, "Here we are... wow, it's a whopper!" But wait a minute, now there's just silence.

Why isn't she crying yet?

More silence, and I panic all over again, even more as a see a pinky, purply, gross little body passed to a midwife holding a towel.

"Is she OK? Is she breathing? Just bloody pinch her OK?" I shout. There's a ripple of laughter, which is quickly covered up by a few coughs. Then that's when I hear it.

First a whimpering that gets louder and louder, turning into a full-blown angry sounding cry as they whip her off to get weighed. I'm crying again, and I realise Henry is crying too and he's stroking my hair, and all of a sudden everything is perfect. Who cares about the horrible house, or a car that only has two back seats, or that Henry nearly missed the birth. He's here now. We're a wonderful family. Henry, Dottie, Arthur, Mabel and baby girl Martha.

"Well, he's a healthy weight that's for sure. Nine pounds and thirteen ounces," the midwife says. "And what a head! There's no way you'd have turned this boy, and he obviously knew it!"

"She!" Henry and I both say in unison, looking at the middle-aged woman who is carrying our crying daughter towards us. The baby is wrapped in an already bloodiedup blanket.

Seriously, how is she allowed to be holding babies if she can't even get the sex right?

"No, definitely not a she," she says smiling. "I've been doing this a very long time, and I can tell the difference you know." She winks as Henry and I glance at each other in confusion. Then, lowering her arms so I can see the tiny, scrunched-up red face, she says, "Congratulations! It's a beautiful bouncing baby boy."

Mothers Ruined hits shelves Autumn 2015!

Printed in Great Britain
by Amazon.co.uk, Ltd.,
Marston Gate.